MY
BABYSITTER
GOES BATS

Ann Hodgman

Illustrated by

John Pierard

iBooks for Young Readers
Habent Sua Fata Libelli

iBooks
Manhanset House
Dering Harbor, New York 11965

bricktower@aol.com • www.ibooksinc.com

Text and Illustrations Copyright © 1991 by General Licensing Company, Inc.
My Babysitter is a trademark of Byron Preiss Visual Publications

Library of Congress Cataloging-in-Publication Data
Hodgman, Ann. My babysitter goes bats.
(My babysitter) "A Byron Preiss book."
p. cm.
[1. Young Adult Fiction—Horror. 2. Young Adult Fiction—Vampires 3.
Young Adult Fiction—Thrillers & Suspense I. Hodgman, Ann, iII. II.
Title. III. Series: Hodgman, Ann. My babysitter.

ISBN 978-1-59687-793-1
2025

MY
BABYSITTER
GOES BATS

Books by Ann Hodgman

My Babysitter Is a Vampire
My Babysitter Has Fangs
My Babysitter Bites Again
My Babysitter FliesBy Night
My Babysiter Goes Bats
My Babysitter Is a Movie Monster

Stinky Stanley
Stinky Stanley Slinks Again
Stinky Stanley, Superhero

Table of Contents

Chapter One. 1

Chapter Two. 11

Chapter Three. 21

Chapter Four. 29

Chapter Five. 41

Chapter Six. 49

Chapter Seven. 57

Chapter Eight. 67

Chapter Nine. 77

Chapter Ten. 87

Chapter Eleven. 97

Chapter Twelven. 103

Chapter One

"Meg, I think my legs just fell off," said my younger brother Trevor.

I leaned over to check. "No, they're still attached."

"They sure feel as though they fell off," Trevor complained. "I can't stretch them out." He kicked the carry-on bag in front of him. "Why do airplane seats have to be so tiny?"

"This is a normal-size jet," I told him. "But it wasn't meant to hold your entire Lego collection. Did you really have to bring *all* your Lego stuff?"

Trevor glared indignantly at me. " 'Course I did! We're going to be away for two weeks, aren't we?"

Hearing this, my mother turned around in her seat. She and Dad were in the two seats ahead of Trevor's and mine.

"It's two weeks of *vacation,* Trevvie," she reminded him. "We're going to have lots of fun things to keep us busy. Skiing, sight-seeing, um, skiing—it's going to be great!"

My brother didn't sound all that convinced. "Well, in between all the fun, I want to do Legos. I bet they don't have any in Drazylvonia. Not even the plain bricks."

Then he changed the conversation. "Anyway, when are we going to *get* to Drazylvonia?"

Mom sighed. "Not too much longer, honey," she said. "Just four more hours."

Four more hours. I sighed, too. We'd been on the plane for four hours already. We were only halfway there. And while I didn't care much whether there'd be Legos in Drazylvonia, I *was* worried about whatever else might be waiting for us there.

My name is Meg Swain, and I'm in seventh grade. It was the beginning of Christmas vacation, and as you've probably figured out by now, my family was on its way to Drazylvonia. My dad was going to be writing a travel article about winter customs in rural Drazylvonia. The magazine he was writing for had paid for the rest of us to go along, too—all except our cat Pooch, who was staying with a house sitter back home in Delaware. If I knew Pooch, he had already figured out a way to trick the house sitter into giving him five meals a day while we were gone.

Don't worry if you haven't heard of Drazylvonia. It's a little country high up in the Carpathian Mountains, and *I* hadn't heard of it until recently myself. But the things I'd heard, I hadn't liked much.

Things like vampires—actual, living-dead, bloodsucking vampires—which Drazylvonia was supposed to be full of. And a castle—Castle Vladestan—with an ancient curse on it, a curse that killed any human who set foot inside the castle. A castle that I was going to *have* to set foot inside as part of a bargain I made with a vampire back home.

I realize that telling you all this isn't the best way to introduce myself. It will make you think I'm crazy right off the bat. But there's no way to go on with my story until I've explained a few things first. I'll try to be quick about it.

For the past year and a half, a vampire named Vincent Graver has been bothering me. He started out as my babysitter (proving that my parents are terrible at choosing babysitters) and stayed on to haunt me.

Every time Vincent turned up in my life, I tried to get rid of him—but it never worked. He always came back, like the blister I get on my big toe when I wear ice skates for the first time each season. Even when he couldn't come back in human form, he managed to reappear some other way. For example, once his spirit took over a stone gargoyle in an ornamental fountain.

I'd battled Vincent for two summers in a row at our summer house on Moose Island, Maine. But a few months before my family's trip to Drazylvonia, at the beginning of this school year, Vincent had turned up back home in Delaware at the same time as my friend Brooke returned from seven months in Europe. She was pale and hollow-eyed, and I got really worried about her. I was right to worry, too. Brooke had been turned into a fledgling vampire during her trip.

After going through a lot of troubles it would be too hard to explain, I persuaded Vincent Graver to make a deal with me. If I went to Drazylvonia and did a vampire errand for him, Vincent would see to it that Brooke was devampirized.

The errand? Oh, just picking a sprig of a Drazylvonian plant called death's-head thyme and putting it into the hand of a vampire prince whose coffin lay in the dungeon of Castle Vladestan, and then escaping from the castle before the sun set. Granted, it wasn't as easy as buying a dozen eggs at the grocery store. Still, I hadn't worried too much about my task. I mean, as long as I got out of the castle before the vampires woke up, I'd be okay, right?

But when I heard that Castle Vladestan was cursed, I got really nervous about the job. No person who set foot in the castle came out alive—oh, I guess I told you that already. Well, you can see why it was on my mind.

Vincent Graver had arranged my family's trip to Drazylvonia. (The rest of the family didn't know that, of course. They just thought Dad got a great writing assignment.) Vincent had also made Brooke normal again—on the condition that she would turn back into a vampire if I didn't keep my part of the deal.

And it wasn't only Brooke who would be turning into a vampire. If I didn't complete my task, I'd become one, too.

I shuddered, suddenly certain that Vincent was watching me. That had to be why I felt so edgy and fidgety. Not only was an ancient curse hanging over my head, but an invisible vampire was studying my every move.

There. Now I've told you. And you don't believe me, do you? Well, you will. . . .

Let's get back to the airplane, where I leaned forward and tapped my mom on the shoulder.

"Is it okay if I get up and walk around for a while?"

Mom and Dad both nodded. I undid my seat belt, struggled past my brother, and took a little hike up and down the center aisle of the plane. There wasn't a lot to see—just a bunch of grown-ups lolling asleep, breathing thickly with their mouths open. How could they let other people see them like that?

And how could they sleep in such creepy surroundings? The designers at DrazAir, our airline, must have been a pretty strange bunch. The plane was carpeted in sleek black. The walls and seats were black, too. The flight attendants were dressed in black, as though they were ready for a funeral. Even the soap in the bathrooms was strange: Each grayish cake was embossed with a tiny dagger. Also, I noticed that the plane was making the most horrible grinding noise as it lumbered along. It sounded as though it was just about to—

"We are encountering some unexpected turbulence," came the pilot's voice over the loudspeaker. "Please return to your—*ulp!*—seats immediately. We ask that you make sure—*ulp!*— your seat belts are securely fastened."

The *ulps* were two scared-sounding gulps he made. They came each time just as the plane dropped through the air— or that's what it felt like, anyway. *Turbulence!* It was more as though a giant had picked up the plane and was throwing it down, over and over. I scurried down the aisle, clawed my way past Trevor, and collapsed into my seat. The plane lurched again. I heard the pilot and copilot speaking rapidly to each other, and then the loudspeaker shut off.

None of the passengers was sleeping now. They were sitting bolt upright, rigid and terrified. I was glad there weren't any babies on board. Trevor and I were the only kids, and at least we were old enough not to start screaming. In fact, Trevor wasn't even paying attention to what was going on. Absorbed in putting together a Lego spacecraft, he only clicked his tongue in annoyance when the plane lurched and shook.

"Oh, my Lord," a woman across the aisle moaned. "I left my purse in the bathroom. I bet the flight attendants will *never* let me get it."

My parents peered anxiously over the backs of their seats at us. "We'll all be fine, darlings," Mom said. "Just put your heads down if—"

A sudden growl from the engine drowned her out.

For the first time, I was sorry I had a window seat. *If I look out the window,* I thought, *I'll have to watch us smash toward the ground. I don't think I can take that.*

I reached up to slide down the window shade— just as a cloud of thick black smoke puffed up outside my window and began swirling around in a wild dance.

Was it a fire? I hadn't paid much attention when the flight attendants had explained how to use the oxygen masks. I glanced up nervously to see whether my mask would come down.

I noticed just then that the smoke was thickening and changing shape. Or, rather, it was forming new shapes.

Faces, to be exact.

The smoke was molding itself into seven ghastly, cadaverous faces in the clouds outside the plane. Long hair streamed out behind each face, and each mouth was open in a silent scream of rage that revealed sharp, pointed fangs.

I forgot about the turbulence. All I could think about now were the seven hideous faces. They were staring right at me. In fact, they were floating closer, as if they wanted a better look. Nightmarish and distorted, they kept coming like evil balloons. I shrank back into my seat, but they moved closer. Frantically I wondered whether they'd come right through the window. . . .

Meg.

I looked around quickly. Who had said my name?

No one on the plane was paying any attention to me. They were too busy bumping up and down in the air, and all the passengers I could see (except Trevor, of course) were frozen into various attitudes of panic.

Meg. We know you are coming.

I glanced back outside. The face closest to my window was moving its lips. No sound came out that I could hear with my ears. But the words appeared inside my brain, and I had no doubt the ghoulish face was the one transmitting them.

Turn back. You will never defeat us.

Now I knew who these seven faces belonged to—the seven vampires in the dungeon at Castle Vladestan. Terrified as I was, I was also relieved that no one else could hear them. It would have been *extremely* complicated to explain to my parents how the faces knew my name.

You will never defeat us, the silent voice repeated. *Turn back and go home.*

Give up, or you are doomed.

HEED THESE WORDS!

The faces in the smoke disappeared. The smoke itself lingered a little longer. Then it swirled into a cloud and vanished as well.

At that moment the plane stopped shaking and once more began flying steadily through the air.

Everyone on the plane started babbling.

"That was the most—"

"My whole life passed before my—"

"Man, I thought we were dead meat for sure!"

"I wonder if the flight attendants will let me get my purse now."

That last was, of course, from the woman across the aisle.

My father turned around in his seat to face me and Trevor. He looked pale and sick. "Are you guys okay?" he asked.

I nodded my head, mute. Sometimes it's easier to lie by not saying anything at all.

"What do you mean, okay?" Trevor asked, looking up from his Legos at last. "Is there something wrong?"

"Well—" Dad broke off. "There *was* something wrong, Trev. But since it doesn't seem to have affected either of you . . ."

The plane was cruising along as though nothing had ever happened. A few seconds later one of the pilots started telling us what landmarks we could see outside the window. A few minutes after *that,* dinner was served.

I've heard a lot of cracks about airplane food, but no meal had ever tasted better to me—because we were all alive to eat it, I guess. The feeling of relief made me so hungry that I even ate the rubbery excuse for a pasta salad.

Of course the flight attendants tried to explain away "the occurrence," as they called it. They said it must have been caused by a sudden storm, if you can imagine anything so lame.

I knew better, though. The vampires in Castle Vladestan were telling me that a battle was waiting for me. And to judge from the show they'd put on so far, I had a pretty good idea that they were the ones who would win.

Which meant that when my visit to Drazylvonia ended, I would be among the ranks of the undead.

Chapter Two

The house loomed ahead of us like an immense, crumbling tombstone. All but one of its windows were dark, and its front door was lit by flickering torches. Above, a pale moon struggled to be seen from behind the dark clouds the wind was shoving across the sky.

"Here is inn," said our cabdriver. He steered the cab up the bumpy road that twisted toward the house.

"Oh, it's so *quaint*," my mother said, "just what I was hoping for. It's perfect for your article, dear," she added to my father.

"You're right," Dad said. "It couldn't be better. Native folk architecture! It's got just the right atmosphere."

"Pardon?" asked the cabdriver. "Inn," he repeated firmly as though we hadn't understood him the first time. "Here is inn." The cab lurched and swerved as we climbed the hill. I could hear our luggage sliding around overhead. The driver had used a rope to tie it to the top of the cab.

"I don't know if I like it in Drazylvonia, Mom," said Trevor in a small voice. From what we had seen of the country so far, I couldn't blame him. It was almost midnight, and our cab ride from the airport had been—well, *adventuresome* might be a polite way to put it.

For one thing, the driver went about a hundred miles an hour along icy mountain roads. We all expected to plunge to our deaths at any minute. And after that plane ride, we had all had *enough* of plunging to our deaths, thank you.

Then, too, flocks of huge black birds—not crows, but some kind of hawk I didn't recognize—kept swooping down at us. Every time this happened, the driver would swerve violently out of the way—which only made the plunging-to-our-deaths problem more frightening.

"What's the deal with the hawks?" asked my brother, staring out the window with interest. Trevor has always been into birds.

"They attack car," said the driver shortly.

"Gracious! They don't have rabies, I hope," said my mother. "Do birds get rabies?"

"No rabies. They no sick. Hate vehicles, only," explained the driver. "Always attack car, truck, tractor."

What kind of a place was this, I wondered? But my dad was smiling. "That'll be a great touch in the article," he said happily. "We're really removed from city life out here, aren't we?"

We certainly were. It was so cold outside, so bitterly cold. Icy fingers of air seemed to reach right through the side of the cab to tickle us. We could hear the wind howling even above the rusty cough of the car engine. The evergreens lining the road were imprisoned in hard, icy snow, and the snow on the road crunched under our wheels.

The countryside was dark and empty—empty of humans, anyway. Except for the moon, I never saw a single light until we reached the inn. And at that point, I would much rather have seen a nice Howard Johnson Motor Lodge sign than a pair of flaming torches stabbed into the snow.

The cabdriver practically threw our suitcases out of the car onto the snow. He pointed toward the inn's front door. "In there," he said. He grabbed the fare from my mother, then shot back into the cab. Before we knew what was happening, he was driving away with a screech of tires and a spray of snow. In seconds the cab had disappeared back into the forest.

We all stared at one another. Then my father cleared his throat. "Well!" he said brightly, picking up a suitcase. "I guess that's what you'd call a local character. Takes all kinds, doesn't it?"

He picked up another suitcase and began slipsliding along the icy path up to the house. After a second Mom picked up another suitcase and followed him. Trevor and I followed *her*. The Swain family was beginning its festive Christmas vacation.

The knocker on the front door was a cast-iron face leering evilly out at us from under a thick coating of frost. A ring through the face's nose was what you were supposed to knock with.

"How interesting!" Mom exclaimed. "I read in one of our guidebooks that Drazylvonians are very skilled ironworkers. I guess this would be an example of that."

"It's certainly an example of something," Dad agreed. He picked up the iron ring and smacked it up and down on the lower part of the face. (If that face hadn't been made of iron, its pointed teeth would have been smashed in.)

A dull clang rang out into the icy air. After the clang, there was silence. Then, from deep inside the house, I heard a kind of shuffling—a shuffling that moved closer and closer to the door. As it drew nearer, I suddenly felt a rush of fear.

"Mom, let's go home!" I blurted out.

It was a stupid thing for a seventh-grader to say. I regretted it instantly. Especially when the door opened and a harmless-looking old man in bedroom slippers peered out at us.

"Yes?" he said faintly.

"We're the Swains," Dad said, reaching out to shake the man's hand. "Here at last. Sorry to be late, but we had some trouble with our flight."

Dad paused. The man was staring down at his extended hand as though he'd never seen such a thing before.

"Uh, the Swains?" Dad repeated it as a question this time. "You were expecting us? We've reserved a bedroom for me and my wife, and a suite for our two children."

"I will see," the man said after a second. "You wait." As if there were anyplace for us to go!

We waited, shivering and stamping in the cold, until the man came back down the hall. This time he was looking cheerful and excited. "Ah, the *Swains*! Famous writers!" he said as if our name had only just sunk in.

"Well, not famous," Dad said self-consciously. "As a matter of fact, this is the first travel article I've ever written."

"You have chosen the most ideal of spots, I promise you. Everyone is sleeping now, but tomorrow you will see how the other guests' faces shine with joy to be here. I am Mr. Prelik, keeper of this inn. Come in, come in! We have been waiting for you!"

He sort of flapped us through the front door and into a tiny room that I guessed must be the lobby. This wasn't as bad as the outside of the inn—just kind of bare and shabby. At one end of the room was a faded sofa and some unmatched chairs in front of a big fireplace. At the other end was a little desk with some keys hanging on nails in the wall behind it. That was about it, except for a last-year's calendar hanging on another wall.

"We have everything you could want," Mr. Prelik was saying briskly. "Skiing, both downhill and cross-country. Ice fishing. Snow dancing. Our celebrated lard pudding for Christmas. Yes, we welcome tourists here."

As he spoke, he took two sets of keys off the wall and handed them to my father. "For your rooms," he said, pointing to one key. "For the outside door," he said, pointing to another. "And for the windows." He pointed to the third key on the chain.

"The windows?" Dad looked surprised. "Why do we have to lock the windows?"

Mr. Prelik glanced uneasily at the one window in the room—which was heavily barred. "It is best," he said. "Wild animals . . ." He gestured vaguely at the darkness outside. "At night they sometimes come too close."

Like the hawks that had attacked our cab . . .

"Well," said my mother, "things certainly get lively after dark around here."

"All the better for local color," said Dad. He turned to Mr. Prelik. "Could you show us to our rooms?"

Before Mr. Prelik could answer, Trevor tugged Dad's sleeve. "Can we get something to eat first?" he whispered loudly. "I'm starving."

Dad smiled apologetically at Mr. Prelik. "I know it's late, but do you think you could bring some food up? Trevor's right. We could all use a bite to eat."

Mr. Prelik nodded fervently. "I could slice some cold *cebliac* for you," he suggested. "It is a local favorite. Sheep's heart. We serve it boiled, with a potato stuffing. Very good."

"You know," Trevor put in, "all of a sudden I feel a lot sleepier than I thought. I guess I can wait to eat until breakfast." He let out one of the fakest yawns I'd ever heard.

"Me, too," I said quickly. There were a couple of candy bars in my suitcase, I knew. I could share them with Trevor when we got upstairs. "Let's just go to bed."

And I hope the beds are more comfortable than this lobby, I added to myself.

They were. The two-bedroom suite Trev and I shared was icy cold, but the beds were everything you think of when you think of a featherbed— thick and cozy with big piles of down quilts on top. Forget the candy bars—Trevor dropped his suitcase and fell asleep on his bed without changing into his pajamas. I managed to change and brush my teeth in our bathroom's tiny sink. Then I conked out almost as fast as Trevor had.

The last thing I saw before I drifted off was my father locking the windows in my room. If any creature did try to break in that night, I was too sound asleep to hear it.

"I'm glad they don't serve sheep's heart for breakfast here," Trevor said happily early the next morning.

"Me, too," I answered. "I never thought I'd be so glad to see boring old cornflakes."

We had just finished breakfast in my parents' room (none of us felt up to facing the dining room yet), and now Trevor and I wanted to explore the inn. Mom and Dad, who just wanted to sit around and drink coffee, told us it was okay. "Just don't go poking into other people's rooms," Mom said.

"Mom! We're not babies," I said indignantly.

"Yeah," said Trevor. "I'm mainly looking for the TV, anyway. Do you think they get cable in Drazylvonia?"

Dad chuckled. "You'll be lucky if they get any reception at all."

"If they have a TV at all," he should have said. Because they didn't.

Oh, they had other things. Things like a smoking room full of stuffed animal heads and bearskin rugs and a rack full of antique-looking guns. Three men in suits were drinking coffee in there and, horribly, smoking cigars at the same time.

"I'm never going in there again," I said firmly. "It stinks. And those poor animals!"

They had a leather-lined library with walls filled with (of course) Drazylvonian books. Trevor pulled one off a shelf and opened it curiously. A great poof of dust rose up into his face.

"They've sure got a weird alphabet in Drazylvonia," he said, coughing.

I bent over to see. "That's not their alphabet. They're some kind of chemistry symbols or something. It's probably a science book."

Maybe, I added to myself. But the strange, twisted characters on the page looked more like hieroglyphs than chemistry symbols. I wasn't sure they had even been printed—they looked handwritten. And were they hieroglyphs or magic spells? Because the longer I looked at them, the more twisted they became. I even thought I saw them begin to wriggle like tiny, evil snakes. . . .

Quickly I closed the book. My imagination was getting the better of me. "Let's go see some other rooms," I said.

It was hard to keep track of where we were going. Not many people were up yet. And I wouldn't say that the people who *were* up had faces that were "shining with joy," the way the innkeeper had predicted. Every dimly lit hallway

looked like every other dimly lit hallway, and the inn was so big that we never came back to the same place twice.

There was a music room filled with instruments that were so coated with dust they looked furry. A ghostlike harp stood in one corner, next to a battered harpsichord. A cello was propped mournfully against the wall, its bow forgotten on the ground. A violin leaned up against the cello like a lonely child. There was also a guitar that was missing all its strings.

"Wow, big tourist attraction," I said sarcastically.

"I wonder how long it's been since someone played any of these instruments," Trevor said.

"A century, I bet," I answered with a shudder. I tiptoed across the dust-carpeted floor and plucked a tentative note on the harp. It sounded tinny and flat. Well, at least there wouldn't be any concerts while we were here.

"Let's go outside," I suddenly said. "We can go for a walk and see the local points of interest."

" 'Local points of interest'?" mimicked my brother. "You sound like a tour guide. But sure, let's go out."

We ran upstairs to get our coats. When we got to the lobby, Mr. Prelik, the innkeeper, was sitting at his desk going over some papers. He smiled absently at us as we passed.

"You are going out?" he asked. "Enjoy yourselves in the fresh mountain air."

"We will," I assured him, pulling open the front door. "We're just going to—"

Through the open doorway I saw what the dark had hidden the night before.

It was a castle on the horizon, black against the gray winter sky.

Some castles are graceful, like pictures from fairy tales. This castle was as blunt as a fist. Its ancient square towers punched the clouds. It stood alone on a flat-topped mountain as if the rest of the landscape had fearfully pulled away from it.

As I've said, the castle was pretty far away. So I don't know how I could tell that it was evil. But I knew.

I stepped back inside. "Mr. Prelik, what's that—that building out there?" I asked, pointing.

For an instant Mr. Prelik shuddered. But when he spoke, his voice was as cheerful as ever.

"That is Castle Vladestan, my dears," he said.

I had known that even before he spoke. This was the vampire castle. Where vampires awaited me. And where I would have to fulfill my promise to my vampire foe, Vincent Graver.

"Wow, a castle!" exclaimed Trevor, who knew nothing about my mission in Drazylvonia. "Do kings live there? Can we visit it? How much do they charge?"

"Oh, no, no, no," said Mr. Prelik soothingly before I could answer. "You must not trouble your thoughts about that castle, little one. You would not enjoy it at all."

Trevor looked astonished. "But why not?"

"It is—it is too old," Mr. Prelik said. (Why did I get the idea he was just inventing that?) "Besides, it is closed to the public. The structure is unsafe. The castle could fall at any moment. If you like, I could suggest other castles in the area. Or some skiing or folksinging—*that* you would enjoy."

He jumped up from his desk, walked quickly across the room, and closed the front door in our faces.

"Now," he said, returning to his desk, "let us choose something more interesting to occupy your time."

Chapter Three

"Something interesting?" We all turned around to see my dad, who'd just come down the stairs with my mother. "We hoped you could give us some advice about a few interesting places to visit, Mr. Prelik. I'd like to start my research today if I can."

"Well, *I* think we should visit Castle Vladestan," Trevor put in before Mr. Prelik could answer. He pulled open the front door again and pointed to the castle on the horizon. "See, Mom and Dad? There it is. It's really cool looking. I've never been inside a real castle before, have you?"

I thought poor Mr. Prelik would collapse from the strain. Here he'd been trying so hard to keep Trevor from visiting Castle Vladestan, and now he was going to have to start all over again with my parents.

He did his best, though. "Castle Vladestan is far less interesting than it appears from the outside," he told Dad. "Inside is mostly dust. Not—not glamorous at all. It would hardly be a place for a famous writer to visit."

"Oh, I'm not looking for glamorous places," Dad assured him. "I think a castle would be a perfect place to start my research."

"But as I was just telling your lovely children," Mr. Prelik continued, "that castle is closed to the public. In fact, there are no roads that go there." He paused, looking puzzled for a moment. "Ah, there is another castle nearby that I think you would enjoy," he said. "I will give you directions there."

Mr. Prelik's other castle turned out to be more suburban-looking than our house in Delaware. Trevor was happy, though, when he found a video game room next to the gift shop. And my father met some people who told him about some better places to visit.

"A message came while you were out," Mr. Prelik told me when we got back to the inn that afternoon. "Voldar Constantin would like you to call him at your earliest convenience. Here is the number, and *there*"—he pointed to an oldfashioned black rotary phone on the wall—"is the telephone."

"Oh, I was hoping Voldar would call!" I exclaimed, walking toward the phone. "I can't wait to see him!"

Now I have to jump back in time for a second so that I can introduce you to Voldar. Voldar Constantin had been an exchange student at my school for the first semester. He had lived at my best friend Brooke's house. Like Brooke and me, he was a seventh-grader, although he was a year older than we were.

For a while I had actually thought that Voldar was a vampire. He looked like one, and he talked in a strange, formal way, and he was much more interested in blood than the average American seventh-grader. But it turned out that Voldar hadn't been a vampire at all. He had just been weird and really interested in scientific stuff.

Nice, though. I had been delighted when he told me he'd be home in Drazylvonia for Christmas. And I was delighted to hear his voice when he picked up the phone. By coincidence he lived not too far from where we were staying and from Castle Vladestan.

"My family was wondering if your family could join us for dinner tonight," he said. "We would like to give you a proper welcome to Drazylvonia."

"I'll ask my parents—they're right here. I'm sure they'll say yes, though."

They did. In fact, Dad loved the idea. I could see he was thinking that a dinner with some native Drazylvonians would be great for his article.

Voldar told me his father would pick us up at seven.

"Great. Thanks a lot," I said. "And, Voldar— you won't be serving *cebliac*, will you?"

He laughed. "I expect we will be able to provide something more to your taste than sheep's heart. *Cat's* heart— now, that is a delicious dish."

"You're kidding, right?"

"Of course. We do not eat cats in Drazylvonia. In any case, my parents are strict vegetarians."

"More roast thistles?" Voldar's father asked my mother.

"Well, maybe in a little while," Mom answered. "I'm fine for now."

"Me, too," the rest of us Swains all said quickly.

"But you have barely touched your cabbage, Meg!" protested Voldar's mother. "Do you not like cabbage?"

"I—I do," I faltered. *But not when it's been wrapped around boiled chestnuts, like this cabbage,* I added to myself. "It's delicious, Mrs. Constantin."

"I am glad to hear that, Meg. For you know, we have a saying in Drazylvonia: 'The plow meets many cabbages, but it cannot taste every cabbage it meets.' "

All three Constantins laughed heartily. All four Swains gave polite, confused smiles.

We had been giving polite, confused smiles all evening, ever since Voldar's father had picked us up in his big old station wagon. Like his son, Mr. Constantin was tall, pale, and superformal; unlike his son, he was as bald as the moon. He had bowed deeply when he met us.

"This is indeed an honor," he said. With that, he bowed us out the door of our inn and helped us into his car. When he had fastened his own seat belt and started away from the inn, he suddenly let out a yelp.

"Are you all right?" Mom asked him, startled.

"Yes. I am merely noticing the sky for the first time. The stars! I have never seen them!"

"You've never seen *stars* before?" Trevor asked in amazement.

"No. I have seen stars, of course. But in this configuration, no. The planets are in alignment!"

"That's nice," Mom said politely.

"No, it is not *nice*, Mrs. Swain. It is utterly astonishing. For when the planets are aligned, cosmic forces are unleashed upon the earth."

"Cool!" said Trevor. "Forever?"

"No, no. For one week only. But it is an event of exceptional rarity. I had read that a planetary alignment was coming, but I had forgotten we were to experience it this year."

Mr. Constantin was staring at the sky so fixedly that I was afraid he might drive off the road.

"See?" He pointed. "That is Jupiter, and there is Venus, and there is—"

The car lurched. "Perhaps you could show us when we get to your house," Dad said hastily. "It's—uh—a little hard to see from the backseat. But I'd love to hear more about this when we get there. Perhaps I could work it into my article somehow."

"Excellent notion," said Mr. Constantin. "This is a most rare happening. Let us hope it is a good omen for your arrival."

Let us hope we get to your house alive, I thought.

We did, and Voldar was waiting at the front door. "Hello, Meg. I am overjoyed to see you," he said calmly. He turned to my parents and Trevor. "Welcome to Drazylvonia. I hope you will enjoy your visit."

"I do, too," my mother blurted out. "I mean, I'm sure we will. And this must be Mrs. Constantin?"

A tall woman dressed in flowing black had just walked up behind Voldar. She stepped forward to shake hands with us. "Come in. Come in," she urged. "Dinner awaits you. Dinner and dancing."

"Dancing?" said all us Swains in unison.

"Folk dancing," Voldar's mother explained. "My husband and I are experts on Drazylvonian folk dancing. We would like to teach you a few of our favorites."

"Oh, how . . . That will be . . ." My mother couldn't finish the sentence. If there's anything she hates, it's dancing in front of people.

Voldar was rolling his eyes. I would never have expected him to do something so normal. But I guess children get embarrassed by parents the world over.

It turned out to be sort of a long night, what with the dancing and the Drazylvonian games (Jump Over the Poker was the Constantins' favorite) and the exchange of folksongs from around the world. (Speaking of parents embarrassing their children, you haven't died of humiliation until you've heard my father singing "If I Had a Hammer.")

Trevor fell asleep on the sofa halfway through the singing. I had to sit through it until Mrs. Constantin suddenly exclaimed, "But, Voldar, you have not shown Meg your room! I am sure she will find your experiments fascinating."

I had seen some of Voldar's experiments back home in Delaware, and *fascinating* wasn't the word for them. *Creepy* was more like it. But I needed a chance to talk to him alone—and besides, his parents were about to sing something called "Boating on the Srvinau Dam."

"I'd love to see your room, Voldar," I said, jumping to my feet.

"I must ask you not to touch any of the fungi, Meg," Voldar said when we were up in his room. He pointed to a basket of shriveled toadstools. "They may look edible, but they are deadly poison."

"Oh. Well, I couldn't have eaten so soon after dinner, anyway."

Voldar's room was so filled with glass tanks and models and notebooks and telescopes and surgical instruments that I couldn't see any furniture. After I had dutifully admired his spider collection and shuddered over his beetle-heart dissections (poor beetles!) and gotten a shock from his experiment on static electricity, I turned to him and said, "I need to talk to you."

"Of course, Meg. Take a seat."

I looked around blankly. "Where?"

"Oh. All right, remain standing. How may I help you?"

"Castle Vladestan," I said. I hated even to say the name. "Would you mind going there with me? I've got to see it as soon as possible, and I don't want to go alone.

"I don't like the idea that the castle's just lying in wait for me," I went on. "But I've got to get there. I can't let anything stop me."

A shadow crossed Voldar's face. "Castle Vladestan is not open to visitors."

"That's what our innkeeper said. But I'm not a visitor. I have a mission, remember? I have to pick some death's-head thyme and put it into the hand of—"

"I remember," Voldar interrupted. "But Meg, I must tell you again that this is too dangerous. No one could accomplish such a thing. Least of all a child."

"I'm not a child!" I said indignantly. "I'm only a little younger than you."

"I am a child," Voldar pointed out.

"Yes, but—well, okay. But children can accomplish plenty. I can't let myself think about how dangerous my mission is. I have to keep my promise to Vincent.

"Besides, I don't want to do the death's-head part right away. I just want to see the castle up close. Kind of get a feel for it."

Voldar shook his head. "You would be better advised to stay away, Meg. But if you insist—all right. We shall visit the castle tomorrow."

"Tomorrow?" I squeaked. "We don't have to go *that* soon. We can wait another couple of—"

"Tomorrow," Voldar interrupted again, his voice grim. "Let us get it over with.

"I am sure that once you have seen Castle Vladestan up close, you will realize that your socalled mission may be impossible."

Chapter Four

"Are you going out, Meg?" my mother asked the next morning.

"Yup," I answered shortly, shoving my feet into my boots. "Voldar and I are taking a walk."

"But, honey, it's freezing!" Mom protested. "Don't you want to wait until it warms up a little?"

Of course I did. But I also wanted to get my visit out of the way.

"I'll be fine, Mom," I promised. "Don't wait for me at lunch. Voldar and I might get something to eat somewhere."

"We won't be here for lunch ourselves," Mom told me. "Dad's taking us to visit a glassblower in the next town. Apparently she makes the most incredible Christmas decorations. Are you sure you and Voldar wouldn't like to come along with us?"

I'm sure I sounded genuinely sorry when I told her no. I'm sure of it, because I *was* genuinely sorry.

Voldar, who was waiting downstairs in the lobby, wasn't all that cheerful himself. "So," he said when he saw me. Then he didn't utter a word for fifteen minutes.

It was a bleak morning, and Voldar had chosen a bleak route to the castle. Or maybe *all* the routes in this country were bleak. Swirls of snow whipped against my face as we walked along the narrow, icy road.

After maybe half a mile or so, the road led us into a forest, where the dark evergreens towered overhead like silent sentinels. The snow died down.

Eventually the trees thinned out, and the road began a narrow trail. In a few minutes we came out of the woods entirely and began stumbling up a rocky slope.

"Are—we—almost—there?" I asked breathlessly.

Voldar just pointed silently upward. "Great," I muttered, clomping along after him.

But at the top of the slope, Voldar finally spoke. "There," he said. And he gestured across a huge, flat, snow-covered plain toward Castle Vladestan.

Castle Vladestan. It stood in the middle of the plain like a toy dropped by an evil giant. Swirling yellow mists rose up around it. A flock of those dreadful black hawks we had seen on our first night swooped and dove at the towers. Hunting for something? What could they find in this weather?

I shivered. "The castle seems to be all closed up," I said hopefully. "Maybe we should come back another time."

Voldar finally gave me his first smile of the day. "The castle is always closed, Meg." Voldar said. "But after all I have put you through this morning, you cannot possibly quit now."

"Sure I can! Try me!"

Voldar paid no attention. "Come," he said simply. "We will advance."

We stepped onto the plain—and the sky turned black.

I stopped dead. Voldar was right next to me, but I couldn't see him at all. "What happened?" I quavered, my voice high and lonely in the dark.

"A sudden storm, perhaps," said Voldar. "Give me your hand."

I kind of patted the air until I found him, and we joined hands. Then we stepped forward again.

One step. Two. A few more. And then the ground began to heat up under our feet.

I didn't feel it at first because of my boots. Then I thought I was imagining things. And then I smelled burning rubber. The soles of my boots were starting to cook.

I stopped again. "Is this a volcano?" I cried.

Voldar's voice was still calm. "This is merely the evil power of the castle itself."

"What are you talking about?" I asked shrilly, jumping up and down. My feet were starting to hurt.

"Castle Vladestan fights off intruders, they say."

"But we're not intruders. We're—we're tourists!"

The castle wasn't listening to me. Right then the earth started to bubble.

"Let's keep going," I said grimly, my determination finally kicking in. "Maybe it'll give up."

Still holding hands, we staggered toward the castle.

All around us strange blue flames began leaping out of crevices that had opened in the snowy ground. They lit the air with a ghastly radiance. Lightning crackled overhead, and a wild rain began to slam onto us. The raindrops hissed and sizzled as they hit the flames, but they did nothing to put them out.

Voldar and I must have been crazy to keep going, but we did. At the back of my mind was the memory of those old fairy tales where the prince and princess are tested by hav-

ing to run over hot coals or swim up rivers of fire. Those
fairy tales always came out okay in the end, didn't they? Of
course they did. . . .

But in those old fairy tales the fairy-tale people never
had to deal with a force field. And a force field was what
hit us next.

Literally hit us, I mean. The air in front of our faces became as solid as a glass wall—a wall that was somehow growing and swelling. It pushed us back, step by slow step. I
could still breathe. I could still push my hands through the
surging air in front of me. But I couldn't fight its power.

Then, for a second, the wall of air seemed to draw itself
back—but only to gather enough strength to slam into Voldar and me with such force that it hurled us back to the
edge of the plain.

We lay still for a few minutes, stunned. "Are you all
right?" I asked, or, rather, coughed, as soon as I got my
breath back.

"I think so," Voldar coughed back.

When we could move again, we painfully got to our feet
and began trying to decide how badly we'd been hurt.

"I was only thinking about how dangerous it would be
inside Castle Vladestan," I said ruefully an hour later. We
had limped to a nearby village and were having lunch at a
little café. "I never wondered whether it would be dangerous to walk toward it."

"Nor did I," said Voldar. "I can now see why so little is
known about the castle. I would imagine that no ordinary
mortal has ever gotten closer to it than we did today." He
was silent for a minute, thinking. "I suspect we will need
help from an outside source to get past the force field."

"What kind of outside source? A bulletproof vest?"

Voldar smiled. "It is too hard to explain without taking you there. When you have finished your soup, we will go."

It was a cave-house, built into a hillside at the edge of the village. Voldar had to bend way down to knock at the door.

"Ahmla, the village seer, lives here," he explained over his shoulder.

"The village what? Voldar, are you taking me to meet some dumb fortune-teller?"

"Ahmla is more than a fortune-teller," Voldar said. "She is—shh, I hear her coming now."

The door opened, and an old, old woman was peering up at us. Tiny and frail, she seemed at first to be nothing more than a pile of scarves and shawls. Then I noticed her eyes—which were burning into mine like hot coals—and I forgot everything else.

Voldar asked a question in Drazylvonian. Without taking her eyes off me, the woman nodded briefly. Then she answered something, which, of course, I didn't understand.

"She says you are in grave danger," Voldar translated, "and she would like us to come in."

For all I knew, I might be in even *graver* danger in that cave. But surely Voldar wouldn't have brought me there just to have some old woman kill me! So I bent down and followed Ahmla inside. This whole day was becoming less and less real to me.

Inside, it was awfully dark. That happens when you live in a cave, I guess. Ahmla, who seemed to have been sitting in the dark before we arrived, lit a few candles. Now I was able to see the room was exactly like something out of a fairy tale. I mean, *exactly*.

There was a stone fireplace in the wall with an iron pot simmering over it. There was a black cat curled up in a basket of wool. There were countless jars and bottles and bowls of herbs and potions and weird-looking ointments. There were sheets of parchment printed with spells (or so I imagined), and spiderwebs in every possible corner, and a wax doll stuck with pins (ick), and . . .

I could go on and on, but I'm sure you get the idea. Really, Ahmla might almost have ordered the whole thing from a fairy-tale catalogue.

She motioned us to stools and sat down at the round wooden table in the center of the room. Then she looked at me questioningly.

"Tell her why you are here," Voldar directed me.

"Well, why *am* I here?" I asked him.

"You need help reaching Castle Vladestan, do you not?"

Oh, yes. I had almost forgotten about the castle. Haltingly at first, and then picking up speed, I began to tell Ahmla about the reason I had come to Drazylvonia. Voldar translated.

Ahmla listened motionless, staring intently at me. Then she leaned forward and picked up my hand.

Palm reading! "I don't need my future told," I said to Voldar.

Somehow Ahmla must have gotten my meaning, for she doubled up with silent laughter. Still laughing, she gasped out a few sentences. "She says she would not dare tell you your future. It would frighten you too dreadfully," said Voldar.

Oh, great.

"She wishes only to tell you about your present circumstances," Voldar went on.

And this is what he told me Ahmla was saying: "The planets are in alignment this week." I remembered Voldar's father telling my family the same thing.

"This means that the one whom you serve"— Vincent Graver, I guess—"is in a strong position to achieve his goal. The omens for that are good.

"You are under his power—is that correct?" she asked. I nodded, and Voldar/Ahmla went on. "You have made a bargain with him, a bargain you must keep or else risk losing everything."

Again I nodded.

"I do not see you accomplishing your side of the bargain. Not unless— No, wait. Now I see how it can be done. Child, there is one who must be helped before you can accomplish your mission. A little brother who is in need."

A little brother? I glanced up at Ahmla, startled. *Trevor* was in need? I certainly hadn't noticed that.

"You must do what you can to help this little brother. If not, your whole purpose in coming here may fall apart.

"I in turn will do what I can," Ahmla went on. "Before you leave me, you and Voldar must eat some herbs to allow you to go through the force field." She was pinching leaves off some dried plants and dropping them into a bowl as she spoke.

I turned to Voldar. "I'm not taking any weird potions or anything," I warned him.

"These herbs are not magic," he assured me. "Ahmla knows the use of every plant in Drazylvonia. She puts together a mixture of herbs depending on what the customer needs. All of us in the village come to her for herbs. Even I, before I left for the United States."

"What were your herbs for?"

"To guard against homesickness, of course."

"Well, okay. I hope they don't taste too awful."

"They do," Voldar said simply. Then he continued with Ahmla's message to me.

"You cannot enter Castle Vladestan without carrying the death's-head thyme in your hand. I will tell Voldar the location of this herb. I will also give you a small amount of unguent."

"Unguent?" I interrupted. Unguent sounded even worse than herbs.

"This unguent is to be rubbed on your temples if at any time you need second sight. But you must use it only in the direst circumstances, or it will stun your senses. Keep the unguent with you at all times. Your life may depend on the sight it gives you."

My life had become one-hundred-percent more complicated in the last half-hour.

"Any questions?" Ahmla concluded.

"One. Two, actually. First of all, why does Vincent want me to do all this?"

"That will become clear in time," Voldar translated.

"Well, okay. I guess. And my second question: What about money?" I asked Voldar. "How much does she charge?"

Ahmla shook her head vehemently. "I cannot accept payment for this," Voldar translated. "To profit from a mission involving Castle Vladestan would be terrible. If you achieve your goal, that is payment enough."

I didn't quite see why, but I wasn't going to argue.

Ahmla turned and ladled out some hot water from the pot over the fire. She poured it into the bowl of herbs she had prepared, stirred it a few times, and then handed me the steaming bowl.

"Very interesting," I said politely.

"No, she wants you to drink it," said Voldar. "These are the herbs to fortify you."

I stared down into the greenish, leaf-flecked water. I also took a big whiff of it, which was a serious mistake.

"Do I *have* to?" I begged like a little kid.

Voldar stared at me seriously. "It would be in your best interest. I will drink some, too, of course."

"Oh, okay." At least it didn't have snakes floating around in it. I held my breath, tipped up the bowl, and quickly drank half of the broth.

It tasted even fouler than it had smelled. My stomach churned, and I can't say I felt especially fortified, but at least I didn't throw up.

Voldar drank his share of the mixture with his usual calm. Then he handed the bowl back to Ahmla, who muttered a few words and turned away.

"She is tired now," said Voldar, "and she wishes us to leave."

So we did.

Chapter Five

By the time I got back to the inn, it was late afternoon. As I watched Voldar's taxi pull away, I was practically choking with guilt. How could I have ignored poor little Trevor the way I had?

He hadn't been acting like "poor little Trevor," it was true. But that was probably because I hadn't been paying enough attention to him. No, I'd just been wrapped up in my own problems, never thinking about my brother. It had taken a Drazylvonian seer to tell me that my little brother needed help. If I had opened my own selfish eyes, I would have seen it for myself.

Well, all that was going to change, thanks to Ahmla. I marched into Trevor's room, ready to be a good sister to him.

"Hi, Trevvie! Where are Mom and Dad?" I asked enthusiastically.

Trevor raised his eyes. "They're taking a nap," he said. "Dad got tired at the glassblower's. He tried to blow some glass himself, but I guess he didn't have enough air or something. He got all dizzy and faint, so Mom put him to bed."

"Great!" I said vaguely. "And what are you doing?"

"Just playing with my Legos. I would think you could see *that*."

"Wow, that thing you're making looks cool! What is it?" I plunked myself down on the floor next to him.

"A space hospital," said Trevor. "Hey, don't touch it! It's—"

Too late. I had already picked up the space hospital, breaking off several pieces in the process.

"Fragile, I was going to say," said Trevor. Carefully he took the hospital away from me and started fixing it. He cheered up once he was working again, though.

"See, Meg, isn't it cool? Here are the hospital beds—they have different shapes for all the different aliens who stay there—and here's the operating room. See all those little tools? And here's the weapons console for attacking intruders—"

Now, *that* was something I could help him with. "Trevor, hospitals don't have weapons consoles," I said. "See, a hospital would never attack anyone. They only take *care* of people. Right?" I was proud of myself for having worked my helpfulness into something Trevor was really interested in.

"So you know what I think, Trev? I think we should turn this weapons console into a . . . into a *medicine* console. Here, let me help." Carefully I detached all the guns and missiles Trevor had attached to his building. "It could be where they dispense all the medicines to all the patients. That would make more sense, wouldn't it? Hey, what are you doing?"

My brother was dumping the whole hospital into a box and getting to his feet, that's what he was doing. "I guess I don't feel like playing Legos anymore," he said glumly.

"Oh. Well, that's okay. That's fine! That's great! I can help you come up with something else to do! How about if we write some postcards to people back home?"

"I was thinking maybe I'd just read a comic book," Trevor said warily.

"Fantastic! Here, let me help find one for you." Before he could say a thing, I was rummaging through his carry-on bag. "Batman? Spider-Man? Richie Rich?" I held a bunch out to him. "I can help you with the hard words if you need it," I added.

Trevor had been reaching out to take a comic when he heard that last offer. He froze in midreach and stared at me for a second.

"Maybe I'll just take a nap," he said. And for some reason, he suddenly did sound tired.

"Are you okay? You never take naps!" I said anxiously. I wanted to show him that I really was listening to his problems. "Here, let me fluff up your pillow for you. Can I get you a drink of water? Or maybe you'd like it if I just sat by your bed until you fell asleep. Or how about a little snack first? I could run down to the kitchen and see if they have anything. Would that help?"

"*I'm not hungry!*—I mean, sorry. I'm not hungry." (Trevor is a very polite boy, even to his relatives.) "I just want to take a nap. And I don't need any help to *sleep.*"

"Well, okay," I said reluctantly. "But at least let me help tuck you in."

"Meg. *Stop.* No one has tucked me in since I was *five years old.*"

The poor kid. He needed me so much that he didn't even *know* he needed me. I hoped I'd be able to help him get over that.

Feeling a little lost, I drifted into my room and gazed out the window. It was late afternoon now, and my window showed the lights of the village a few miles away. I was glad I didn't have a view of Castle Vladestan. For at least a little while, I didn't want to have to think about—

Scritch. Scritch-scritch. Scraaaaable scritch.

What was that?

It was definitely some kind of animal. I would have said it was a mouse, except that it didn't sound as though it was in my room. And surely there couldn't be any mice living outside at this time of year; they'd freeze.

Still, the sound was coming from somewhere near me. I stepped closer to the window and peered out. Darkness was coming on so fast now that I could hardly see. But I didn't think there was anything on the ground.

Scritch.

As I watched, a shadow edged its way onto the window-pane—a shadow so tiny it couldn't have frightened even a coward like me. I leaned forward to see what it was.

It was a baby bat.

Considering my history, I have good reason not to like bats. But this one was different.

Not counting his wings, he was about two inches long—maybe smaller than that. His underside, which was all I could see, was a pale, pearly gray. He had a tiny fox face with a twitchy nose. His wings looked like miniature leather umbrellas sewn to clawed feet.

And—I looked more closely—wasn't one of his wings hurt? It was crooked, somehow, as though he hadn't been able to fold it up properly. Yes, he was definitely dragging it. Sort of limping with it . . .

"Oh, you poor little guy!" I said aloud.

When the bat heard me, he flinched and froze. Then, very slowly, he turned his head to peer into my room. When he saw my face so close, he flinched again. But his enormous round eyes didn't turn away.

I'm not claiming I'm psychic or that I understand animals' hidden thoughts or anything. But I knew—*knew*—that that baby bat was asking for help.

"It's okay, sweetie," I crooned. "I know a lot about animals." I really did, too. I've been reading wildlife books for years. "Now, let's see how we can open this window without scaring you away."

It wasn't easy. I had to slide up the sash very gently so as not to jostle the little guy. I was afraid that he would suddenly get scared and either fall off or fly away. But he managed to stay put, though I could see he was trembling.

You have to move very slowly with a wild animal, so I knew I couldn't grab him. Instead, I held out one finger toward him and waited.

The little bat waited, too. My hand was starting to ache from being held in such an awkward position. "Come on," I whispered. "You can do it. I won't hurt you."

I waited more. Finally the bat began to edge slowly toward my finger. When he was close enough, he tentatively touched my fingernail. He patted my fingertip, then timidly climbed aboard.

Very carefully I brought my hand back inside and closed the window with my other hand. The bat was wrapped around my finger like a fuzzy pipe cleaner. I ran a finger down his back—and realized right away how cold he was. The first thing I had to do was try to get him warmer.

Gently, I scraped him off my finger and into my cupped hand. Then I tiptoed into my brother's room.

Trevor really *was* taking a nap, which was perfect. I needed to borrow one of his Lego boxes for the bat, and if he had been awake he might have claimed he "needed" it.

I picked up the smallest box I could find, slid the Lego pieces out onto the floor, and brought the box back into my room. There I lined it with some tissues and tried to put the bat back inside.

By now, though, he didn't want to let go of my hand. Baby bats ride around on their mothers' backs, and I guess this little one instinctively felt more secure holding onto something.

"It's just for a few minutes," I said soothingly. "You'll be even warmer this way. Besides, if your wing is hurt, I shouldn't be jostling you around too much." I picked him up by the scruff of his tiny neck and put him into the box. Then I folded a towel, put it onto the radiator, and set the box on the towel. Now the baby would be warm without getting too hot.

"Food," I went on, thinking aloud. "Milk with sugar in it. Or maybe he's weaned? What if he's eating insects now?"

But how would I find bugs in the dead of winter? How could *he* have been finding them? Come to think of it, how could he have been *born* in the dead of winter? Didn't bats hibernate? I was almost sure they did.

Obviously there had been some mistake in this little bat's timing. And since I didn't much like the thought of feeding him live insects, I decided to try the milk first.

I covered the bat's box with another towel and ran down to the kitchen to heat up some sugared milk.

When it was ready, I ran back upstairs. The bat was curled up in one corner of his box, already looking more alert.

I found a cotton swab in my suitcase, dipped it into the milk, and touched his nose with it.

The little bat sneezed and licked the milk off his nose— and a shiver ran through his whole body. He grabbed the swab and began lapping at the milk-drenched cotton as hard as he could.

I must have dipped the swab in the milk thirty or forty times before the bat had finally had enough. I could actually see his stomach growing rounder now. Gazing woozily up at me, he pushed the swab aside and lay down again. In a second he was sound asleep.

"You are the cutest thing in the whole world," I said softly, stroking his velvety fur. The bat snuggled down under my hand and let out a tiny sigh.

"Trevor!" I called softly. "Wake up and come see what I've found!"

Chapter Six

"Can't you leave Batboy here with me?" Trevor asked the next morning. "It's too cold for him out there."

"It's too cold for him in *here*," I said. "If the heat goes off in my room, he could freeze to death. I'll keep him inside my shirt pocket."

You've probably figured out that Batboy was the name of the baby bat. Don't blame me for the name—Trevor thought it up. Batboy had spent a comfortable night in his box, and he was feeling very happy now. He had even started squeaking when he saw me. Or maybe he was squeaking at the sight of the Q-Tip. Anyway, I knew he'd get to like me once he associated me with his meals.

I wasn't sure what to do with his wing. I hoped that if I could keep him from moving around too much, it would heal on its own. That was another reason I wanted to take him with me. In my pocket, he wouldn't be able to open his wings at all.

"Where are you going?" asked Trevor.

"Voldar's taking me on another walk." I shivered. Today we'd be hunting the death's-head thyme, which meant that afterward we'd be heading back to Castle Vladestan, which meant that after *that*, I'd probably never come back.

Thinking of that reminded me I should still be trying to help Trevor. It wasn't fair to him to let my own concerns get in the way of my relationship with him.

"Want me to help you brush your teeth?" I asked. It was all I could think of at the time.

He glared at me as if I were crazy. "I've already brushed them," he said shortly.

"Good for you!" I said brightly. Trevor gave me an even more suspicious look. "Maybe I could help you clean up your room, then."

"I like it messy."

"Well, that's fine," I said heartily. "That means we'll have more time to talk before you guys leave." That day Dad had planned a trip to an ancient monastery whose monks supported themselves by making coffee cakes for Christmas. Trevor hadn't wanted to go, until Dad told him that visitors got to lick the huge bowls where the batter was mixed.

"What're we going to talk about?" Trevor asked.

"Oh, feelings and stuff. How have you been feeling lately, Trev? Anything you want to tell me about?"

My brother is usually pretty calm, but something about this question seemed to irritate him.

"Yes-there's-something-I-want-to-talk-about!" he said in a rush. "What I want to *talk* about is, why are you being such a dip all of a sudden? Are you trying to earn a Girl Scout badge or something?"

Stay patient, I told myself. *He needs your help, remember? He just doesn't know it.*

I forced a smile. "I'm sorry if I'm coming across like a dip," I said in my nicest voice. "It's just that I thought this vacation would be a good time for me to get to know you better."

"Why? We're not getting married."

"But we never get to see each other during the school year. And, anyway, you seem awfully worried lately." *That* was a total shot in the dark. But if Ahmla said he needed help . . . "I just wondered if there was anything I could do to make you feel better."

"Meg, I don't want to make you feel bad yourself. But I'm okay. Really I am," Trevor told me. "The only thing I'm worried about is why you keep trying to act like Mom."

"Because you're my little brother, and I care about you."

I ran for the door before Trevor could hit me.

The day before, another guest had told us that the inn had a car service. Mom and Dad gave me permission to use it.

"Within reason," Dad said, "which means you can't drive to London without telling us. And you can't use it alone. But if you and Voldar want to do some sight-seeing together, that's fine."

I decided that "sight-seeing" certainly included picking up Voldar at his house and then driving to the spot where Ahmla had said we would find death's-head thyme growing.

"There is a spot at the edge of a stream in the woods behind Ahmla's home," said Voldar. "Ahmla says we should be able to find a few sprigs of thyme there."

"But won't it be dead? I mean, it's about a million degrees below zero."

"Death's-head thyme grows best in snow in cold weather, Ahmla says," Voldar told me. "It thrives on hardship."

The inn's driver, I could see, did not thrive in cold weather. He certainly didn't like the idea of driving us to the edge of the woods and waiting for us. But I promised him we wouldn't take long. I saw him pull out a Drazylvonian newspaper as we headed into the woods, so I knew that at least he'd have something to do while he waited.

"We can't stay long, anyway," I told Voldar as we started into the woods. "Batboy needs a feeding soon."

"Who is—Batboy, did you say?"

When I explained, Voldar seemed astonished. "There is at this moment a small *bat* in your pocket? Meg, have you considered the possibility that he may be rabid?"

"Of course he's not rabid," I scoffed. "He doesn't act sick at all. I don't think he even has teeth yet."

"But this tame behavior sounds most abnormal—" Voldar broke off. "Ah, this must be the stream."

It wasn't "streaming" at the moment, of course. It was frozen black and solid and lifeless. I couldn't imagine how any plant could survive at this time of year.

But then I noticed a bit of gray-green vine poking out from under a snow-covered rock on the bank. I pointed it out to Voldar. "Is that what we're looking for?" I asked.

"Yes. Ahmla said it grows under rocks. Let us push this one aside and see what we find."

"What an attractive plant," I commented as we both strained to dislodge the frozen rock from the frozen ground. "It grows under rocks in the dead of winter. There. I think it's moving a little."

The next second the rock tumbled down the bank and crashed onto the ice. Where it had lain, there was a tangle of flattened vines covered with small, pointed leaves.

"That's death's-head thyme?" I asked Voldar. "It looks so—so boring!"

"You will not say that when you touch it," Voldar answered grimly.

When I reached out to pick a sprig from the tangled mess, I saw what he meant. The thyme's pointed leaves spiraled straight through my glove and jabbed into my skin. They felt quite a lot like needles—the big, thick embroidery kind.

"Ouch! This is horrible!" I exclaimed. "It's *just* the kind of thing a vampire would use to send a message. I'll have to carry it in my pocket—my jacket pocket, Batboy," I said quickly in case he was listening from inside my shirt pocket. "Don't you worry. I won't let these nasty old sharp things come near *you*."

"She has lost her mind over a species of vermin," Voldar commented to no one in particular.

Back at the inn, though, Batboy managed to charm even Voldar. "You are right, Meg. Clearly he does not have rabies. Perhaps I could carry him in *my* pocket when we go to Castle Vladestan," he suggested hopefully, dangling a milky Q-Tip in front of the tiny bat's face. "I believe my shirt is warmer than yours."

Naturally I said no. Anyone who called Batboy "vermin" did not get to carry him no matter *how* sorry he was.

"Another walk, honey?" Mom asked at lunch. I had invited Voldar to eat with us. "What are you going to see this time?"

Voldar jumped right in. "I would like to show Meg the ancestral home of some famous Drazylvonians," he said. It was certainly true enough.

"Hey, I'd love to see those!" Dad exclaimed. "Mind if I come along, too?"

Luckily Mom gave him a leave-the-kids-alone glance—and Dad sank back down in his chair. "Wouldn't Trevor like to go along, at least?" he asked.

I tensed in my seat, but luckily Trevor said no. "Today I want to make a space hospital *by myself*," he said, casting a dour look in my direction. That was fine with me.

You've already heard what the plateau the castle sat on was like. The difference this time was that we were able to walk across it up to the castle with no difficulty—unless you count my heart beating so hard I thought it would burst through my chest.

Castle Vladestan didn't look any more welcoming when we got close to it. I had never seen a more menacing place. As Voldar and I stared up at it, I couldn't think of a single joke to lighten things up.

The only things growing around the castle were thorny hedges, bare of leaves. Bones—I hoped they weren't human, but they looked it— littered the ground around the castle. The building didn't even have any windows; it was smooth, icy stone all the way to the top. Its towers were topped with dozens of iron spikes. ("The better to impale you, my dear," I could imagine the vampires saying.) And its curved iron-barred door had no handle.

"How are we supposed to get in?" I asked faintly. "No, Batboy," I added, reaching into my jacket to tuck him back in my pocket. "You stay put."

"Perhaps the death's-head thyme opens the door for us," suggested Voldar. "Why not try?"

Reluctantly I pulled out the canvas bag of thyme I had brought with me and carefully started to lower my hand into it. I wasn't really looking forward to getting the door open. I almost couldn't help hoping we had picked the wrong kind of plant.

"Batboy, no!" I said again before I could pull the thyme out. He was wriggling so frantically in my shirt pocket that I was afraid he'd hurt himself.

All of a sudden he climbed out of my pocket. "Here, Voldar, hold the thyme," I said, thrusting the bag into his hands. "The bat's running around on my stomach. Ouch! His claws are scratching me right through my shirt!"

I was patting myself all over, hoping I could get hold of Batboy as he scrabbled around under my jacket. But in gloves my fingers were too clumsy to work very fast. Before I could get the jacket off, Batboy suddenly darted up my ribs and came out through my collar. He flinched as he felt the cold air, but still he climbed up—and out—until he was perched on my shoulder. He was squeaking wildly and trying to flap his wings, as though he'd take off at any second.

"Oh, no! He'll hurt himself!" I cried frantically. "Get him, Voldar!"

Quickly Voldar stepped forward. But before he got there, Batboy launched himself into the air— and immediately plummeted to the ground.

The poor creature let out a little shriek of pain. His left wing was now dangling out at a crazy angle, but it didn't stop him. He started pulling himself rapidly along the ground toward the castle.

I bent down to pick him up, but Batboy was too fast for me. He skittered right up to the castle and leaped up its wall. Then he began racing back and forth along the stones, his nose twitching furiously.

As calmly as I could, I moved toward him. "Come on, Batboy," I said soothingly. "It's too cold for you out here, and you'll hurt your wing even more, running around like that. Let's get back in my shirt, where it's warm."

Batboy paid no attention to me. He ran along the castle's smooth surface until he reached a minuscule crack between two stones, then squeezed through the crack and disappeared.

"Oh, no," I said. I rushed forward and tried to peek into the crack, but I could see nothing.

"Let him go, Meg," said Voldar quietly. "He obviously wants to be free."

"How do I know that? He's too little to be free!"

"He is quite independent," Voldar pointed out.

I bit my lip. "Okay. You're probably right. But I don't care. Voldar, he's still drinking milk, for heaven's sake! I've *got* to get him. I can't just leave him in there."

I felt so frustrated that I pounded the stones with my fist. "Open up, you stupid wall!" I yelled idiotically. "Can you give me a hand, Voldar?"

Just then, one of the stones moved beneath my fist.

Not much—but enough for me to see that it was *supposed* to move. It wasn't just crumbling. It was actually sliding inward.

"Wait a sec," I said. "I think this may be some kind of passageway. Come help me push."

Voldar was already at my side. The two of us pushed as hard as we could.

With a strange groaning, the stone moved back. So did the stones under it. Before us was now a channel about a foot deep and one stone wide— where once the wall had been smooth.

"We must push again," said Voldar. "Harder."

The stones resisted for a second before the channel deepened.

All of a sudden it slid back another foot, then glided smoothly out of our way.

We were standing before a narrow, open passageway into the castle itself.

Chapter Seven

"Okay, Voldar," I said. "Go on in."

"This is your mission, Meg," Voldar said politely. "I would not think of going in before you."

It might have degenerated into one of those endless no-you-first-no-you-first arguments, except that I suddenly remembered Batboy. I ran through the passageway without another thought.

Which was probably why I didn't see the long, curved sword pointing straight at me until it was too late.

The sword, which was hanging on a long chain at the end of the passageway, just sliced through the sleeve of my coat.

"Whoa!" I said, leaping backward. "Voldar, be careful! They're armed!"

"Who is armed?" Voldar asked, coming up behind me in the passageway. "Oh, I see what you mean. This is an excellent example of an old Drazylvonian scimitar. A rather primitive way to keep out intruders, would you not say?"

"It worked pretty well on *me*," I said dryly. "Now, let's see what else they have in store for us."

The passageway opened into a larger chamber, which was, of course, completely dark. No windows, remember?

I could tell it was large by the echoing of our footsteps. "We'll have to bring a flashlight with us the next time we come," I said.

If there was a next time.

"I do have a box of matches in my pocket," Voldar announced. "I always carry them in case of an emergency. We must conserve them, but—" He lit one and held it high over his head.

What was that?

A hideous monster was leaping toward us, its bloody claws outstretched and—oh, no, it wasn't. It was just a tapestry on the wall of the round stone chamber. An awfully realistic one, though. Somehow the claws had been fashioned to come right out of the fabric. When Voldar lit another match, I leaned closer and saw that the claws had been sewn on, and that red knots of thread were "dripping" from them.

"Pretty good sewing," I commented as casually as I could. "I wouldn't have something like this in my living room, though."

"I do not feel that this is a living room," Voldar said quietly. "Look over there." He lit a third match, and I saw the array of metal implements that could only have been torture devices. My imagination wasn't running away with me this time, because I had proof. A human skeleton was stretched out on one of them. . . .

"Blow out the match," I said shakily. "I've seen enough."

You may have seen enough, the castle seemed to answer, *but you haven't heard enough.* At that moment the most dreadful wailing rose up all around us. It sounded like the shriek of someone in pain, plus the grief-stricken wail of someone who had lost a child, plus the feverish sobbing of someone desperately ill, plus the terrified scream of someone who was about to die.

I know, I know. A noise can't hurt you. But you've never heard this noise. It was an unbearable sound, and just when it climbed to its highest pitch, something jumped onto my head.

"No!" I howled. "No! Voldar, I—"

Whatever it was sprang onto my shoulder, scrabbled down my collar, and climbed into my shirt pocket.

"Oh," I said into a sudden silence. "It's Batboy!"

I could feel him trembling against my chest, and hear his tiny squeaks of fright. The squeaks were cute in comparison to the scream, but I knew how upset he was.

"Where have you been?" I asked, reaching into my jacket to pat him. "Why did you come into this terrible place?"

As if in answer, the wailing began again.

I couldn't stand it. I stumbled across the room, frantically patted my way toward the passageway, and raced out into the real world.

Luckily, Voldar was right behind me. Later, I'm sure I would have felt guilty to think I had abandoned him in my moment of panic.

When we were safely outside, I turned to him. "Voldar, I'm giving up," I said. "I don't care how babyish it sounds—I can't take any more of this."

Voldar eyed me sternly. "You have a mission, Meg," he reminded me. "And those things in the castle—however frightening—were nothing more than special effects."

"Yeah, right. It's easy to say that when we're outside," I told him bitterly. "Anyway, forget my mission. *Nothing* is worth going back into that castle. For the rest of my

life I'll—I'll just have to live with the fact that I'm a coward."

Voldar didn't say a word.

We got back to the inn safely. I sent Voldar home in the inn's car. I ate dinner with my family and went upstairs early, leaving my parents and Trevor poring over some old Drazylvonian children's books in the library.

A Drazylvonian couple was already having coffee in the library when we got there. "Are American girls always so quiet?" I heard the woman ask as I headed toward the stairs.

No, not always. There just wasn't anything to say.

In my bedroom, on the bedside table, was a little vase of flowers. I jammed the death's-head thyme into the vase.

"No sense letting it die, I guess," I said to Batboy. "At least I've got you back. That's the only good thing about today."

I tucked him into his box on top of the radiator. "Why on earth did you go into the castle in the first place?"

Batboy looked up from his cotton swab to squeak at me, but that was his only answer.

When Batboy was all settled down, I changed into my pajamas. I was putting my jeans on a chair, when something small fell from one of the back pockets and hit the floor with a little clang.

"Oh, it's that unguent Ahmla gave me!" I said aloud, picking it up. (Batboy was good company even if he couldn't answer.) "I'd forgotten all about this."

The unguent was in a tiny, flat tin about the size of a man's thumbnail. I pried open the lid and looked inside.

The dab of gunk in the tin looked like nothing more than a bit of grease. It didn't even smell.

"How's *this* stuff supposed to help me in emergencies?" I asked Batboy. "I bet it's not magic! It's probably just hand lotion." I dipped my finger into the stuff and stirred it around discontentedly.

Batboy, who had been dozing in his box, let out a shrill squeak. He sat upright, staring fiercely at me.

"What's the problem?" I asked him. "This isn't dangerous! I'm sure it isn't anything! Ahmla's probably a fake."

Just to *prove* she was, I rubbed the grease into both temples and snapped the tin closed. "See?" I said to the bat defiantly. "Nothing's happening. Boy, *this* stuff will sure come in handy when—"

A flash of lightning seared through my brain, and I fell backward onto my bed.

At first there were just random words. Then they swirled together into a message, a message that pounded around and around in my head like cars on a racetrack.

You will die. You will die. You will die. . . .

Now I could see a vision of myself, gray as clay, dragging along a deserted stretch of road.

You will join the ranks of the undead.

Yes, that was what I would look like, I realized—a vampire. A vampire who hadn't had any blood in a long time. Watching myself (if you know what I mean), I could see how desperate I was getting.

And then, in the vision, Vincent Graver—the vampire who had started me on this terrible journey—joined me on the road.

He looked exactly the same as when I had first met him. White faced. Hollow eyed. Dressed all in black, with bloodred talons instead of fingernails, and dark red lips through which the tips of his pointed teeth were showing.

On his face, though, was an expression I had never seen before:—sad and disappointed and angry all at once. And there was a touch of pity on his face, too—pity for me. As if he didn't want me to suffer the way I was going to suffer now.

You failed, Meg, I heard him say. I kept falling onto my knees, but he never reached out to help me up. *You let me down. Now your life is mine.*

The Meg in the vision stared feebly up at him. *You could have done it yourself,* I protested weakly. *You didn't need to send me.*

I could not return to earth in a human form. You know that— you caused it. (A long time before, I had taken away Vincent's chance of being able to come back in a body—his own or anyone else's. Score one for me, even though it wasn't going to do me any good.)

I knew the planets would be aligned—the best time for me to achieve my goal. You were the logical person to carry out my mission, since I could not. And remember, Meg—the idea of a trade was yours, not mine. . . .

I gazed blearily at him. *What was your goal, anyhow?* I asked. *You've never exactly told me.*

It is simple enough, Meg. Another vampire has usurped my role as prince of my vampire circle. I want to conquer him and take back what is mine. Then I will reclaim my full vampire powers.

Oh, so I'm your go-between! I asked sarcastically.

Precisely. Not that you have been spectacularly successful so far. Handing a small bouquet to my rival should not have been so difficult.

Well, it can't be the first time the planets have been aligned, I said with the ghost of my old spirit. *Why did you have to wait for me? Why couldn't you have tried to get your powers back before this?*

Outside commitments always prevented me, Vincent replied.

In quick succession, he sent me several images of himself.

In one image Vincent was tied to a tree and surrounded by a circle of angry peasants holding torches.

In another, he was being buried under a mountain of stones by a howling mob.

Then he was being nailed up inside his coffin and thrown overboard, and then he was being burned at the stake, and then—

Stop, Vincent! I cried. *Don't show me any more!*

A strange, sad flicker of emotion emanated from Vincent. *As you see, Meg, some people are even less tolerant of vampires than you. Throughout history, most humans have never particularly liked those who are—different.*

Yes, I knew that. Most humans don't even like *humans* who are different—let alone vampires.

Now I see why you couldn't go back yourself, I said.

No, he said dully. *Only you could. And you did not. And now—now you must pay.*

Another series of images streaked through my head. I saw myself, the real Meg, turning on my parents and Trevor. Sucking their blood while they slept, and gradually turning them into vampires. Turning even my poor cat Pooch into a vampire, so desperate was I for blood.

Then came some kind of holiday party. All our relatives were invited. We had invited them only because we needed their blood. As our huge, happy family sat around a long table, we fell upon them like wild animals. Screaming, they tried to escape, but we had locked all the doors. . . .

You win, I said to Vincent. *I'll finish the mission.*

I fell facedown into the road.

It was Batboy who woke me up. He had crawled out of his box and was nudging my hair. His claws tickled.

"Stop it, Batboy," I mumbled, sitting up in bed. I scooped him up into my hands and held him against me. "Thanks for waking me, though. That was the worst nightmare I've ever had."

Batboy let out another one of his shrill squeaks. Angrily he dug his claws into my hand.

"Ouch! Cut it out!" I said. Now he was scolding me furiously, like a squirrel, and practically dancing in my hand.

"What is it? What's the matter?"

As if he couldn't stand it any longer, the bat scrambled out of my hands and skittered across my bedside table. He planted himself next to the tiny tin of unguent and—I swear it—stamped his foot at me.

"The unguent? What about it?"

Suddenly I remembered Ahmla's warning. If the unguent was used when it wasn't needed, it would stun a person's brain.

Surely what had just happened to me had stunned mine.

"You're telling me it was the unguent that made me see those things," I said slowly. "Not a nightmare."

Batboy chittered excitedly. He almost seemed to be nodding.

"The unguent gave me that vision. So I guess— so I guess that unguent works. Is that it?"

Again the bat chittered.

"And my vision showed me what would happen if I don't go back to the castle and do what I'm supposed to do."

Batboy made a little purring sound.

"So I have to do it," I said sadly. "I can't get out of it. The consequences are too terrible for me, my family, and Brooke."

Now the bat climbed back across the bedside table and snuggled into my hands. I wondered if he was trying to comfort me.

Then it dawned on me that I'd just been having what amounted to an actual *conversation* with Batboy.

"I can't believe this," I gasped. "Y-you understand what I'm saying, don't you?"

He stared up into my eyes, and I could see that he did.

"You're not a bat, are you?"

I could tell by his eyes that he wasn't.

There was someone in there. Someone—a person? a soul? the victim of a spell?—was trapped inside this bat's tiny form.

"Are *you* the person who needs my help?" I whispered.

He stared into my eyes for a long, long time, and I saw that he was.

In the morning I happened to notice the little vase of flowers on my bedside table. The death'shead thyme had turned the other flowers completely black.

Chapter Eight

"The mission's back on again," I said when I called Voldar the next morning. "I changed my mind. I'll tell you why when I see you. Would you—would you mind going back to the castle with me today? I want to get this over with."

There was a long pause.

"Oh, okay," I said quickly. "I understand. I'm asking too much."

"No," Voldar said just as quickly. "It is not that. I most absolutely will come with you. But I have to go somewhere with my parents this morning. I will not be able to go with you until afternoon. Would that suit you?"

"Sure!" I was so grateful that he wanted to go with me that I would have let him come at midnight. Then I remembered something. "I'm supposed to do this thing in the hour before sunset anyway," I told Voldar. "That's what Vincent said when he first told me about this. So late afternoon would be best."

"I will be there at two o'clock," Voldar promised. "The sun sets early this time of the year, so dress extra warmly. How late do you think we will be out? I will need to tell my parents something."

That was something I hadn't considered before. Mom and Dad certainly wouldn't like it if I stayed out after dark without telling them. They would hate it even more if I never came back, I had to remind myself.

"Gee, it could take a while," I said. "We'd better come up with some kind of story, don't you think?"

"I do think so," Voldar answered. "And actually, the timing is quite good for us. Tonight and tomorrow night, as soon as the sun sets, there will be a tremendous meteor shower in the northern sky."

"You sure have a lot of weird planetary stuff in Drazylvonia," I commented. "Planets in alignment, meteor showers—the works. Well, what about this meteor shower?"

"Simply this. It is quite famous. Each year at this time, people climb high into the mountains to watch it. It happens in other places, too, of course, but this is the best place to see it. Perhaps we could tell your parents that is where we will be?"

Perfect. My parents wouldn't get upset if they knew we'd be with a lot of people. Well, if they *thought* we'd be with a lot of people.

In fact, when I told them about it, they decided to come along and bring Trevor. Dad's article, you know. Local color, and so on.

"Yes, you definitely must go," Mr. Prelik assured them when they asked about it. "People come from all around to watch the meteor shower. We are preparing delicious box dinners for all the guests who wish to see the show."

"Don't bother about making one for me," Trevor said quickly. "I'll just bring along some cereal." So far, there hadn't been a single Drazylvonian food he had liked.

"Meteors are shooting stars, aren't they? Maybe I can work in something about the Christmas Star in my article," my father said, making a note on his hand. He never remembers to carry notepaper with him.

I was a little worried about having my family tagging along, and Mom must have noticed. "Meg, I bet you and Voldar would like to watch the meteor shower on your own, from a different part of the mountain," she suggested. I don't know if she thought we needed romantic privacy or what—but if that's what she thought, I certainly didn't bother setting her straight.

"Sure, Mom," I said. "How late can I stay out?"

"Until you get bored with the meteors, I guess," Mom said cheerfully. "I trust you to be responsible."

By one o'clock in the afternoon I was so nervous I couldn't do anything except pace around my room talking to Batboy.

"It's going to be all right. It's going to be all right," I kept muttering unconvincingly. "This is all going to come out fine. Vincent wouldn't have given me this job if I didn't have a chance of doing it. Or a pretty good chance, anyway . . . It's going to be all right. It's going to be all—"

"What are you doing, Meg?" Trevor had been watching me from the doorway without my noticing him. "Why are you walking around in circles like that?"

"Trevor! You didn't hear what I was saying, did you?"

Wow, that was a great way to keep a secret. "I mean, I—I was reciting some poetry. Some sort of, um, *poetry* with, you know, lines in it. It's a little embarrassing, actually."

"I can see why," said Trevor. "You're getting weirder every day, Meg. Anyway, I was wondering if you could help me with something."

My heart sank. "Oh, Trev, I'd love to, but this isn't a good time. I'm about to leave with Voldar, and—"

"Meg! For fifty million *days* you've been going on and on about wanting to help me! Now, when there *finally* really is something you can do, you say you won't! It's only going to take a second. I promise you'll be able to start walking around in circles again in just a couple of minutes."

What could I say?

"It's this Lego castle," Trevor said when we got into his room. "See, I just can't get it to look right. Can you help me make it better?"

"Gee, Trev, I think it's fine! I really do!" The last thing I wanted to do was work on a *castle*. I wanted to be ready to leave the minute Voldar got there.

"I don't think you need to do anything to fix it. Actually, it's one of the best things you've ever made." I was already moving toward the door.

"You promised," said Trevor severely.

"No, I didn't," I said, but I sat down again. At least helping him might make the time pass a little faster.

"You need some turrets," I said. "Here, we can use these pieces for turrets. And what about a drawbridge?"

"Cool!" agreed Trevor. "See, I knew you could help me with this!"

I had been right. Playing with my brother did turn out to be a good distraction. So good, in fact, that for the first time that day I didn't notice what time it was. The phone rang to let me know Voldar was waiting for me downstairs.

"Oh, no! It's two-thirty!" I wailed. "Trevor, I'm sorry, but now I really do have to go."

"Okay," said Trevor peaceably. "Do you want me to babysit Batboy while you're gone? I'm not going to the meteor shower until later with Mom and Dad. I bet he'd be happier here with me."

"No way! I mean, no thanks. He can come along with me. I bet he'll like watching the vampire shower. I mean, *meteor shower.*"

Without waiting for an answer, I dashed into my room to get my things.

The sun was low in the sky by the time we finally reached the castle. My forgetting the death's-head thyme and having to go back for it slowed us down even more—and then we had had to fight our way through people starting their way up into the mountains for the meteor shower.

It was very cold out, just as Voldar had warned. Luckily I had thrown on an extra pair of long johns. I didn't like the way the sky looked. It was a strange, menacing green with pale, glowing streaks running through it.

"What's the matter with the sky?" I asked nervously. "It's not sunset *already,* is it?"

"Oh, no. That is the way the sky always looks before a meteor shower," Voldar told me. Very nicely, he didn't remind me that it was my fault we were late. And he had remembered to bring a flashlight along—another thing I hadn't thought about. I had been in such a hurry, I'd completely forgotten how dark the castle would be.

I remembered when we got there, though.

"I can't remember which stone we pushed to get in," I said. "Can you?"

Voldar was staring at the castle with an equally blank expression. "No," he said at last. "Should we just try until we find the right one?"

I couldn't stand the thought of having to press against all those ice-cold stones, but what other choice did we have?

Then I remembered Batboy, who was still in my pocket. I reached inside my jacket and pulled him out.

"Can you do your stuff for us again, cutie?" I asked. "We need to get into the castle."

This time, though, Batboy didn't seem to want to help out. He hunched up in my palm and tried to put his head under his wing. It was so much colder now that the sun was setting that I couldn't blame him. But we had to get going.

"No, Batboy. No." I jostled him a little. "We really have to do this."

Voldar was staring at the two of us in astonishment. "You believe he understands?" he said.

"I know he does," I said firmly. "He's just pretending. Come on, Batboy." I walked over to the castle and showed him the stones. "Show us where the crack is."

Obediently he crawled over the stones until he found the tiny crack between two of them. He paused there for a minute, shivering, and looked up at me. "Is that all?" he seemed to be asking.

"Good boy," I said warmly. "You can come back inside now."

The bat was in my pocket again before I took my next breath.

I turned to Voldar. "Ready?" I asked. Silently the two of us began to push against the stone.

I had sort of been hoping it wouldn't work this time, but in a few minutes the passage was silently inviting us— daring us—to go inside again.

Voldar aimed his flashlight inside. There was the scimitar, waiting for us at the end of the passage. We pressed up against the walls and slid past it into the chamber.

Now Voldar played the flashlight slowly across the torture machines, across the clawed tapestry, and all around the room. We could see no sign of another passage.

"The vampire coffins are downstairs, Vincent told me. How're we supposed to get downstairs?" I asked just as the wailing moan we had heard the day before started again.

This time I just stood there, waiting for it to end. When you were expecting it, it wasn't quite as bad.

"Look." Voldar shone the light over the torture machines. "Is that not a hole in the floor?"

Yes, it was. A round hole in the stone floor, about two feet across and just underneath the skeleton's grinning head.

"Maybe we are meant to climb into it," Voldar suggested.

Oh, no. I couldn't. I *couldn't*. "Let me have the flashlight for a minute," I said.

No room has ever been inspected as carefully as I inspected that one. But in the end I realized that Voldar was right. The only way we had to get downstairs was to climb down that hole.

Get tough, I reminded myself. *Remember what will happen if you don't.* Still holding the flashlight, I marched across the room and aimed the beam down into the hole.

"It's slimy, Voldar," I said with a shudder. "The—the tunnel walls are all green and oozy."

Voldar had reached my side by then. "Yes," he agreed, "but there are stairs cut into the walls. Clearly we are meant to climb down."

"I can see that as well as you," I snapped. "Here, you take the light and shine it down for me. Then you can throw it down and I can shine it up for you."

I held the flashlight out to him. Unfortunately I accidentally dropped it before he touched it.

We stood there, dismayed, as the flashlight clattered down the hole and smashed on the basement floor—and went out, of course.

"I have some matches left," Voldar said from somewhere in the pitch dark. "I will light one when we are downstairs. Now go, Meg. And be careful."

"I'm going," I quavered.

And I let myself down into the hole.

There can't be anything worse than climbing down a slimy tunnel into a pitch-black dungeon. Especially when you're the first person climbing down, and you don't know what's waiting for you. All that slime was slippery, too. A couple of times I almost lost my grip.

I'm going to fall down and hit the stone floor and die, I thought with horror. *No one will ever find me. No one will ever see my body. . . .*

Sternly I reminded myself that even *that* fate would be better than the one waiting for me if I didn't help Vincent.

At last my foot touched down—and I stepped into something squashy. Was it the floor of the dungeon? No, I didn't think so. It seemed to he some kind of fungus. I swallowed hard and pulled my foot out of it.

"I'm down," I called up as cheerfully as I could.

And Voldar started carefully down the stone stairs.

When Voldar was down, he said, "Now let us look and see what awaits us here."

I heard a rustling, and then the little hiss of a match being struck.

In the few seconds before the match went out, we saw that water was dripping from the ceiling. There were no windows, so we would never know whether the sun had set or not. Burned-out torches on the walls must once have been the room's only light.

"Do you think we can light a torch?" I asked, patting my way along the wall until I found one. "Here, let's try."

Luckily there was still some kind of wick left in the torch. When Voldar touched a match to it, the wick sputtered and smoked—but after a couple of seconds a thin, wavering flame appeared. Voldar plucked a second torch off the wall and lit it from mine.

Now we could see more than we wanted.

Everywhere there were grim signs that people had once been imprisoned here. Chains and manacles were fastened into the walls. A couple of dirty bowls lay on the floor next to some of the manacles—food for the prisoners, probably. I hoped that they had all been set free and lived long and happy lives. Somehow I doubted it.

At last I aimed the torch into the center of the room.

Voldar caught his breath sharply.

Yes, there were the seven coffins Vincent had told me about. They were placed at intervals around the room, like beds in a dormitory.

"I believe this must be the vampire prince's coffin," said Voldar in a shaky voice. He was pointing to the largest one. "Do you see?"

Now I did. There was a glass window in the top of the coffin, and through it we could see that a vampire was definitely inside. He did not look friendly.

Voldar took a few steps backward and passed a trembling hand over his eyes. "Surely that must be the leader," he choked out. "There could not be a more frightening looking one."

"No."

The time had come.

I lifted the lid of the coffin.

There were the vampire's red-clawed hands, folded on his chest. I turned quickly away from them.

It would take only a second to do what I'd come to do—give him the message from Vincent.

Trembling, I cautiously pulled the thorny sprig of death's-head thyme out of the bag and jammed it into the vampire's folded hands.

With a roar he sat up in his coffin.

Chapter Nine

"I—I'm very sorry," I stammered, trying not to meet the vampire's pale, furious eyes. "I didn't mean to wake you. I mean, Vincent didn't *tell* me that the thyme would wake you. I thought it would just—well, I apologize."

I was sort of babbling now, and I kept glancing longingly at the tunnel that led back upstairs. "I guess we'll be going so you can get back to sleep, okay?"

There was an ominous creaking from the six coffins that were still closed. Then, slowly, in different stages of yawning and stretching, the other vampires sat up as well.

Even in my panic I had time to notice a couple of things about them. They were all different ages, for one thing. The youngest looked younger than Vincent, the oldest more than ninety.

They were dressed in different styles, as though they had come from different eras. The vampire prince's black suit and black cloak were very much like Vincent's. The youngest vampire—a grayish-skinned girl of about fifteen who had stringy blond hair—was dressed in a burlap gown that was almost medieval. The oldest had the ruffled doublet of a Renaissance man.

One thing all seven vampires had in common, however, was that they were staring at me. (The female vampire was eyeing me suspiciously, for some reason.) It was not a comfortable feeling. As I looked at them I realized that these were the same awful faces I had seen out the window of the airplane—the ones that had told me to turn back.

"I didn't realize I had summoned *all* of you," I said, stunned.

"You did not summon any of us," the prince of the vampires corrected me coldly. "The sun went down. This is the time we rise from the dead and move about the earth."

Oh, no. This was what playing with Trevor's Legos had brought down on my head.

"Well, all the more reason for us to be leaving," I said. "You've probably got lots of stuff to do, and we wouldn't want to get in the way." *In the way of your fangs*, I didn't say out loud.

"Why did you place the death's-head thyme into my hand?" asked the head vampire. "Do *you* intend to wrest vampire control from me?"

"Oh, my gosh, no!" I giggled idiotically. "I was just doing a favor for a—a person. A vampire, actually. He asked me to give you a message, kind of."

"Which vampire was this?" the head vampire asked, though I was sure he knew already.

"His name is Vincent. Vincent Graver."

The six vampires sat entirely still.

"I see you did not heed our warning," remarked the head vampire calmly. "Vincent Graver is our eternal foe. That you are his servant does not bode well for you."

"Oh, *that* warning," I said, remembering the ghastly faces I'd seen from the airplane window. Well, I'm not really his *servant*," I said. "I just kind of owe him a favor. You see—"

"We are not interested in your paltry explanations," interrupted the oldest vampire, the one in the ruffled doublet.

I bit my lip and shut up.

"We would be interested in an explanation from *you*, however," Voldar chimed in. I was amazed at how calm and levelheaded he sounded.

"Why should we explain anything about ourselves, when you serve our enemy?" the vampire prince asked.

"We are not servants," Voldar corrected him, "merely messengers. Clearly we have chosen to ally ourselves with the wrong side in this battle. Perhaps if you tell us a bit more about yourselves, we might be able to serve *you* in some way."

Good thinking, Voldar.

But the vampire prince didn't seem convinced. "Why should I trust either of you?" he asked.

"You have no reason to trust us," Voldar replied calmly. "Still, your tale is no doubt an interesting one. As a long-time resident of Drazylvonia, I would be interested to learn more about the history of this region—a history in which you have no doubt played an illustrious part."

If there was such a job as being a vampire diplomat, I was sure Voldar had it all sewn up.

The vampire prince bowed slightly. "You speak well, human. For this I shall humor your request—"

He hadn't glanced at me in all that time. I hoped he was forgetting about me.

"And then I shall dispose of you," he continued.

Now I really hoped he would forget about me.

"Know, first of all, that my name is Boris, and that I am of an ancient vampire family. Each of my companions here represents an honored vampire lineage.

"However, Vincent Graver's family is even older than the rest, and they possess certain powers other vampires lack. The ability to move about in daylight is one such power. As long as they avoid direct sunlight, they can survive. Still, though they have been our leaders since time immemorial, they have always been an odd group."

And when a vampire calls another vampire odd, I suppose he must be *incredibly* odd.

"They are fonder of ideas than most of us," chimed in one of the younger vampires. "More fanciful, you might say, and less practical."

"Who is telling this story?" asked the head vampire sternly. "To continue—because of his ancient lineage, Vincent Graver was chosen to lead the vampires of Drazylvonia."

"Who led them before that?" I asked.

"Vincent's father."

"What happened to him?"

Boris glanced expressionlessly at me. "A regrettable accident. A group of peasants put a stake through his heart. We exacted revenge, of course."

The way he said it made me sick to my stomach.

"This happened shortly before Vincent reached the age of sixteen. Every vampire has a preordained age, you know, and when he reaches that age, he stays there forever."

"Why?" Voldar asked.

Boris shrugged. "It is the way, that is all. We do not question it. But Vincent had a brother whose preordained age was much, much younger. He reached the age of three and never matured after that."

Batboy stirred in my pocket. I hoped he would come out of this adventure alive.

"Stunted, he must have been," remarked one of the vampires.

"Something wrong with his mother, no doubt," added another. "It would have been better to drown the runt at birth."

Boris fixed them with a stern glance, and they quieted down.

"The brother—whose name was Grebiv—was of course irritatingly immature. And not only that, he showed no signs of normal vampire behavior. From babyhood on, he refused to sample human blood. He claimed he did not like the taste," Boris said in disgust.

"Nor would Grebiv attack animals, though his parents patiently showed him how again and again. He lacked blood lust entirely. He was utterly harmless. Sweet, I believe you mortals would say." Boris sounded even more disgusted now.

Grebiv sounded nice to me, but of course I didn't tell Boris that.

"What does Vincent have to do with this small brother?" asked Voldar.

"Nothing," Boris answered. "But it was deemed wrong for a vampire leader to have such a relative in his family. We asked Vincent to get rid of his brother before he, Vincent, took over the leadership of our brethren."

"Get rid of him!" I said indignantly. "Get rid of him *how!*"

"How he did it was no concern of ours," said Boris. "The fact is that he refused to do it at all."

Good! I thought. It was the first nice thing I had ever heard about Vincent.

"I was angry. After all, it was not as if Vincent were being asked to rid the world of a being of consequence. But he was much more obstinate than any of us had expected. I then decided to take matters into my own hands," Boris went on. "I would destroy little Grebiv myself.

"Since he ate human food, I knew that terminating his food supply would end the creature's life quite swiftly."

"The creature!" He sounded as though he were talking about a spider or something!

"It would have been simple enough to keep Grebiv locked away from food until he had wasted away to nothingness. I lured him to a suitable spot in the castle and closed Grebiv up behind a wall.

"There, he could have remained secure," said Boris. "Vincent's rise to power would have been smooth, and in time he would have forgotten Grebiv."

"Maybe," the female vampire whispered.

"However, he did not forget his brother. He searched the castle until he discovered Grebiv one night. He set the little idiot free. And in the morning, when I was sleeping in my coffin, Vincent attempted to drive a stake through my heart.

"Luckily, the sun had only just started to rise when he attacked me so fiendishly. The other vampires heard my cries, woke up, and came to my rescue.

"Naturally we met to determine Vincent's fate. Vincent stubbornly insisted that he had been right to attack the attacker of his brother. It was decided that Vincent's attack on me was proof that he was unbalanced. A vampire must not let his family interfere with his responsibilities to the community. Thus Vincent Graver was clearly unfit to rule us.

"Accordingly, Vincent was banished from Drazylvonia. I became prince in his stead," Boris finished simply.

"What happened to Grebiv?" I asked.

Boris shrugged. "We never saw him after his brother had been banished. Probably he perished without Vincent's care. Good riddance to a worthless existence."

"Indeed," echoed the other vampires.

There was a little pause. Finally—bravely— Voldar broke it.

"A fascinating history," he said politely. "Thank you for enlightening us."

Boris didn't answer. He was frowning and staring off into the distance.

"He is nearby, is he not?" he asked slowly. "I sense his presence."

"Who?" Voldar and I asked in unison.

"Vincent."

Voldar and I stared at each other. "If he is, I don't know anything about it," I finally said.

No answer.

"I don't! I promise you!"

I began backing slowly toward the stairs. "If— uh—if Vincent *is* around, then maybe Voldar and I should leave so you guys can work things out."

"Oh, we will indeed work things out." The planet Pluto could not have been colder than Boris's voice. "But there is something else to do first. We vampires have a saying, you know. A saying that I believe you mortals have often used throughout your wretched history."

"A saying," I repeated wonderingly. "What saying is that?"

Quicker than I could have believed possible, Boris leaped forward and clasped my wrist in his icy hand.

" 'When the news is bad,' he quoted, 'kill the messenger.'"

Chapter Ten

This would probably have been a good time for that unguent Ahmla had given us. After all, it was supposed to be used in the most dire circumstances. And these particular circumstances had to be the direst we would ever see.

With my free hand I patted my pockets desperately. I was pulling backward as hard as I could. I knew I had brought the unguent with me—but where was it? It had to be somewhere!

Boris was slowly bringing me closer to him. He opened his mouth in a demonic smile. His long, curved fangs sprang into view. For a panicky second I was afraid he was going to bite me.

Then, as he let go of my wrist to seize my neck with both hands, I realized that it was worse than that. He was going to strangle me.

His hands squeezed with merciless strength. I gasped for breath, but it was useless. The edges of my vision flickered and turned black, and in a second I knew I'd pass out completely. . . .

Voldar saved my life. Later, he told me that he had torn open his backpack the instant Boris grabbed me. He pulled out a head of garlic—and rammed it into Boris's roaring mouth.

Garlic! Why hadn't I thought of that?

It slowed Boris down for only a minute, but that minute gave us the time we needed to reach the tunnel. Unfortunately the six other vampires had set out after us by then.

"Halt!" Boris howled. "If any of you venture from this chamber, I will destroy you! Vincent's messenger belongs to me alone!"

The other vampires fell back obediently.

Up the slimy ladder we clambered, Boris breathing heavily close behind us. Now we were in the torture chamber above the dungeon.

And the second we got upstairs, our torches blew out.

I swallowed a moan of fear. Surely Boris could see in the dark better than we could. Making noise would only help him find me faster. I hoped that somehow the same thing would occur to Batboy.

What could we do? *What could we do?*

Oh, Vincent, I thought in despair, *can't you help us somehow? You didn't tell me this would happen!*

"Why should I have told you?" I could imagine him telling me mockingly. "We are deadly enemies, are we not? I owe you nothing. Nothing at all."

That was true.

Holding my breath, I tried to melt backward as quietly as I could. I felt a lot better when I touched the wall behind me. My eyes had adjusted to the dark now, and I thought I could see the passageway that led outside. If I moved very, very carefully, maybe I could reach it.

Or maybe I should keep close to the tunnel. Wouldn't Boris expect me to be going toward the passage?

Yes, staying near the tunnel probably made the most sense for the time being. I wondered if Voldar had had the same idea. I wondered if there were any other good vampirc-warder-offers in Voldar's backpack. I wondered where Voldar *was*.

Out of the darkness came the sound of Boris breathing, and I felt a quick surge of relief. He sounded as though he was across the room from me. If I could just stay put and outwait him, maybe he wouldn't find me.

"I know what you are planning," he said. (Yes. I was right. He was across the room.) "Let us wait, then. We can make it into a little game. Time means nothing to me. I am prepared to wait forever. The instant you move, I will be upon you."

I don't know how long I did stay put, but it must have been hours. Certainly they were the longest hours of my life. My muscles were screaming before ten minutes had passed, and I was shaking uncontrollably. If I hadn't been leaning against the wall, I'm sure I would have fallen over.

Also, I had to go to the bathroom quite badly. This is not the kind of thing people think about when they imagine themselves in mortal danger, but I can assure you that it does happen.

If I could just wait it out until sunrise! Would fate be that kind to me?

No. Just when I was starting to think I might be able to outwait Boris, Batboy decided to climb out of my pocket.

Of all the times to do it! Slowly, slowly the little bat crept up toward my neck. His claws were tickling me, but for once I felt no urge to laugh.

What are you doing, you little dope? I thought frantically. *Get back down!*

He wasn't going to. He reached my collar, hesitated for a second, and then silently crept out onto my shoulder.

I had always thought that breaking out into a cold sweat was just a figure of speech. Now I realized that it wasn't. Batboy was probably hungry. In another second he would start squeaking. Then Boris would know where I was, and it would be all over.

Batboy nuzzled me once. Then I felt him stretch up, the tip of his good wing brushing my cheek.

He was getting ready to fly—with only one wing. I didn't dare try to hold him back. Moving my arm would make my coat rustle.

I closed my eyes and hoped he didn't crash to the floor.

With a leathery flap of his wings, Batboy vaulted into the air. It sounded as if he made it. He was flying. His injured wing must have gotten better.

As Boris sprang toward the sound, I realized that Batboy had taken off toward the passage that led out of the castle. At least he'd be free. But for a fleeting moment I felt sad that he'd left me behind.

Boris thundered toward the passage. I heard a clanking sound: He must have brushed against the chain holding the scimitar.

Then I heard another sound. It was the scimitar itself.

And it was slicing through something thick and wet-sounding.

Boris let out a monstrous bellow, but the sound stopped abruptly.

Something hit the ground with a sickening *splat*.

Then came a thud as something much larger hit the ground.

Then came silence.

And *then* came a tiny, trembling child's voice.

"Vincent?" the voice piped up nervously.

"I am here, Grebiv," came Vincent's voice. A second later a glow lit up the passageway—and Vincent himself—my vampire babysitter—walked into the castle, torch in hand.

"Vincent!" I gasped. For a crazy second I felt like hugging him. "How—how did you get here? And in your body?"

"With Boris's destruction I am restored to my full powers," Vincent said, and waved his torch toward the floor. I saw Boris lying there in two parts: head and body. The scimitar was swinging triumphantly over him. On the far side of the chamber I could see Voldar leaning against the wall.

Next to Boris's body stood a tiny, frightenedlooking little boy.

No, not a little boy. A little vampire, maybe three years old.

He was wearing a black romper with a little black lace collar and black high-button shoes. Someone had taken a lot of trouble to dress him nicely. I wondered if it had been Vincent.

When the little vampire saw who was carrying the torch, he rushed up and flung his arms around Vincent.

"Who are you?" I said, though I was sure I already knew the answer.

"He is my brother, Grebiv," said Vincent. He leaned over and patted the tiny boy on the head. "That was good work, little fellow," he said softly. "You killed him."

"He did? How?" Voldar whispered.

"I flew onto that knife thing," said the little boy. "I swung it back and forth as hard as I could. When it—went through, I stopped being a bat."

"Sweet," Boris had called Grebiv in disgust. I hoped that, somehow, Boris realized now that Grebiv was much tougher than he had ever realized.

"I—I'm cold, Vincent," said Grebiv shakily. "When I was a bat, I had fur, but now I'm awfully cold."

Vincent whipped off his cape and wrapped it around his brother. "It is too long," he said, "hut I will carry you."

"Here, give him my scarf, too," I said impulsively. "It's nice and warm, and that cape is too big around his neck." I was happy to see that his arm looked just fine. I was glad that I had helped it to heal when Grebiv was a bat.

I pulled off the scarf and handed it to Vincent. He seemed surprised as he took it.

"Thank you, Meg," he said. "Thank you as well for taking such good care of my brother. I will never forget it as long as I live."

And Vincent was immortal, so that was a pretty long time. "He was fun to take care of. I'll miss him," I answered wistfully. "What are you guys going to do now?"

"Well, first we must ensure that none of the vampires downstairs causes further trouble," Vincent replied.

"What about Boris?" croaked Voldar. He hadn't spoken in so long that his voice wasn't working too well.

"I hardly believe further action will be necessary in Boris's case," he said.

"But, Vincent," I blurted out, "you've been killed lots of times before, and you always came back!"

"True enough," said Vincent. "However, this castle will shortly be crumbling to pieces. Boris will be hard put to reunite his head and body when he is crushed under several tons of rubble."

"Oh, that's good," I said without thinking. Then— "*Crumbling?* How do you know?"

"I have spoken a charm that will destroy it," said Vincent calmly. "Now that I rule the vampires of Drazylvonia once again, I would like to begin my reign from a new location. One that is free from the taint of Boris and his henchmen."

It seemed strange to hear one vampire referring to another vampire as tainted. I mean, *all* vampires seem kind of tainted to me. But I guess Vincent had his own standards—and if I had had to choose between him and Boris, I would certainly have chosen Vincent.

"I spoke the charm before setting out to come here. The castle will topple shortly," said Vincent.

As if to answer him, there was a faint rumbling under our feet.

"I must hurry downstairs to complete my work. And you two must hurry outside. I would not wish *you* to be crushed under several tons of rubble. Goodbye," he finished abruptly.

"Goodbye? You can't say goodbye yet!" I protested. "You haven't even *started* to explain what's going on! How did you get here just in time? What did your brother eat until I fed him? Where will you go now? What—"

"I am sorry, but there is no time for this, Meg," said Vincent. He honestly did look sorry. The floor was starting to shake, I realized. "I must dispose of Boris's companions. Run, now. Save yourselves. I will never require your services again."

"But—" I started to say.

Then I felt Voldar's hand on my arm. "We must do as he says, Meg," said Voldar. "Come. Immediately."

"But, Vincent, won't you and Grebiv be crushed, too?" I asked, hearing my voice rise hysterically.

"We will be all right," Vincent replied. "Do not worry about us."

Voldar started pulling me toward the passageway.

Everything was happening too fast. I yanked myself away and turned around, desperate to ask Vincent a few more questions—to see Grebiv one last time. . . .

But they were already gone. And now the whole castle was shaking.

"Goodbye!" I called.

A huge rock wrenched itself from the ceiling and smashed to the ground only inches from my face. Another, then two more, were right behind it. Smaller stones and dust began raining down onto the chamber floor. A huge crack suddenly appeared in the wall next to me, flowering out rapidly into a lacework of smaller cracks—

"Meg!" Voldar shouted urgently. "Come *now!*"

I had to do as he said. The ground was now pitching so hard we could hardly remain on our feet. Together we staggered out of the passageway, and then we ran. We ran as far from the castle as we could. Then we heard a terrible roar—and turned around just in time to see Castle Vlades-tan collapse in on itself.

The impact threw us both to the ground. A choking cloud of stone dust rose up thick around us, making it impossible to breathe. I buried my head in my arms, and I'm sure Voldar did the same.

For a few seconds I lay there. *I can't believe this*, I thought, dazed. Behind me, the rocks were still churning as they set-tled, and the ground was still shaking.

I struggled to my feet. No sooner had I lifted my face from the ground than a curve of brilliant flame swooped toward us. Then another, and another—

"It is the meteors, Meg," said Voldar, pushing himself to a stand. He chuckled weakly. "In all the excitement, I had totally forgotten the meteor shower."

I got to my feet and stared with wonder at the sky. Above me, streaks and curls and sprays of blue-white fire were turning the dark sky into an explosion of light.

"They—they can't hit us, can they?" I whispered.

"No, no," Voldar assured me. "They burn up before they reach our atmosphere."

"But they seem so close," I protested.

"They are countless miles away. Truly, Meg." Voldar reached out and patted me on the shoulder. "Much farther away than the dangers we have just faced. The time for fear is over. Let us return home."

And we began our cold journey back to the inn, while overhead the sky whirled and blazed insanely.

Chapter Eleven

My parents were sitting in the lobby chatting with a few other guests when I finally dragged myself through the front door.

"Hi, Meggie! Weren't those meteors fantastic?" Dad asked.

I stared stupidly at him. "The meteors," I repeated. "Yes. Yes, they were very exciting."

"Are you okay, Meg?" My mother was obviously concerned. "Has something happened?"

"No, no." With an effort I forced my sagging face into a smile. "I'm just tired."

"But you're all dirty, honey!"

"I fell a little bit, coming down the mountain." Suddenly I yawned so hugely that the woman who'd been talking to my mother looked shocked.

"Is it okay if I sleep in tomorrow?" I asked, yawning again.

"Sure, honey," said Mom, "if that's what you want."

"Good. See you later, then."

It was only eleven o'clock when I went to bed, but I slept for fourteen solid hours.

My father woke me the next afternoon. "Voldar's on the phone," he said. "Shall I tell him you're not up yet?"

"No, that's okay," I said groggily. "I'll be right there."

"H'lo?" I croaked into the phone.

"Meg. You sound like a frog," said Voldar.

I smiled. "I feel like one. What's up?"

"I am," Voldar said, "and I was wondering if you felt like having breakfast."

"Breakfast? It's one in the afternoon!"

"Come to my house for lunch, then," said Voldar.

"That sounds great," I said. "And after that, can we go see Ahmla? There are a couple of things I want to ask her."

Ahmla looked as though she had been expecting us. She patted me on the shoulder and took the leftover tin of unguent from me without a word. I had finally found it in my coat pocket when I'd gotten back to the inn.

She motioned me and Voldar to sit down. Taking a seat herself, she looked at us expectantly.

"We should tell her what happened yesterday," Voldar said.

"She doesn't already know?"

"Perhaps, but it would be more polite to speak than to make her guess."

So we told the long story and Voldar translated while Ahmla sat motionless.

"I feel almost sorry that Batboy turned out to be Grebiv," Voldar said at the end of our story. "I liked him the way he was."

"Me, too," I said. "But he was happy to be back to normal. I could tell. And that reminds me of one of the things I've been wondering about. Can Ahmla tell us how Grebiv turned into a bat in the first place?"

"I can do better than that," Ahmla answered through Voldar. "I can show you."

She picked a skillet up off her stove and went outside for a minute. When she came back in, the skillet was filled with hard-packed snow.

Ahmla put the skillet on the table. Over it, she ladled a little hot water from the pot in the fireplace. As the snow melted, it formed a hard, glassy coating on top of the skillet. Humming a strange, twisting tune, Ahmla fanned the skillet with her apron—and the glassy coating turned into a picture of Grebiv and Vincent playing together.

This was a Vincent I had never seen. For once he looked almost nice. He wasn't exactly smiling, but his expression was pleasant, and he was being very attentive to his younger brother as they built a snow bat in the moonlight.

Then the scene changed. Now we saw Vincent indoors quarreling furiously with the other vampires. Grebiv huddled, frightened, in a corner. He was rolling a little rock around and trying to look as if he thought it was fun.

Boris gestured angrily at the little vampire, and I knew he was telling Vincent to get rid of him. Vincent shook his head vehemently. Soon the two of them were shouting at each other. Then Vincent suddenly swept Grebiv into his arms and stormed out of the castle. The rest of the vampires began muttering ominously.

Now we saw Vincent carrying the little boy to a cave set in the hillside.

"Your cave?" I asked Ahmla in amazement.

She nodded, and began to speak to Voldar.

"My cave, but this is when it belonged to my many-times-great grandmother. This took place many generations ago, remember. Vincent asked her to help protect the child," Voldar translated. "He feared for his brother's safety—

feared Boris would attack Grebiv someday when Voldar was not watching. My ancester knew that adult vampires can change into bats at will, but Grebiv was too young for this. So she transformed him herself."

She gestured to the ice's mirrorlike surface. In it, Grebiv—Batboy—was wobbling wildly around the room, testing out his wings. Vincent was watching him with a look of mingled pride, relief, and worry. Behind him a woman who looked almost exactly like Ahmla was also watching. I couldn't see her expression.

"Her spell was meant to last for as long as little Grebiv was in danger," Ahmla said. "Who was to know that Vincent would be banished by the other vampires and wander, homeless, for so many centuries?"

The scene shifted to Vincent storming angrily out of the castle again. But he was not carrying his brother this time.

"The little one never learned to fly very well," said Ahmla sadly. "During Vincent's final confrontation with the other vampires, Grebiv wandered off. He was not seen again."

We could see Vincent walking through miles and miles of woods, calling out his brother's name. We saw him transform himself into a bat and soar off into the night to look among the other bats flying through the sky. But he always came back alone.

"Vincent has been alone on this earth for hundreds of years," said Ahmla softly. "Vampires are solitary creatures by nature—but a vampire without kin is lonely indeed."

I knew I wasn't supposed to feel sorry for Vincent. We were total enemies. But I pitied him now. I couldn't help it.

"Now that Boris is vanquished—" Voldar began.

But Ahmla shook her head. "Do not say that," she warned. "He is halted for now, yes. And for now, Vincent is leader again. But the balance of power could shift at any time."

"Do you mean Boris could come back?" I asked, appalled.

Ahmla nodded.

"Without his *head?*" I squealed.

"Vampires can reconstitute their bodies in a number of ways," said Ahmla. "But let us not dwell on that now. For the moment, Vincent is in control."

"And what about Grebiv?" asked Voldar. "Will the brothers stay together from now on?"

"Yes, indeed. Would you like to see?"

We nodded eagerly, and once again Ahmla shook her apron over the sheet of ice.

The ice wrinkled, then became smooth again. In its new picture, meteors were blazing through the air—nature's fireworks raining down on the peaceful landscape. A glittering curl of sparks shimmered above the ruins of Castle Vladestan, then vanished.

Two bats—one sleek and large, the other small and fluffy—crawled out one of the narrow window slits at the top of the ruined castle. They looked at each other for a second, then launched themselves into the sky.

One flew cleanly, his flight swift and sure. The other could hardly fly at all. Mostly he just dipped and hobbled through the air. But whenever he seemed about to fall, the larger one flew to his side and caught him. After a while the little bat's flying became steadier.

The two bats circled three times above the castle—and then they were gone.

Chapter Twelve

"Meg, did you ever find your scarf?" my mother asked on the morning we were packing to leave Drazylvonia.

I shook my head. If I'd told Mom the truth— that my scarf was keeping a baby vampire warm— she would either have thought I was crazy, or she would have said, "Well, go get it, then!" And I certainly had no plans to track it down anytime soon.

"Oh, well," said my mother, shrugging, "it's one less thing to pack."

I couldn't believe it was time to pack already. The rest of our visit to Drazylvonia had been so much fun—so much nice, ordinary, regular fun— that I actually wished we could stay longer.

With my mission out of the way, I'd been able to have a real vacation. Voldar and I had gone skiing a few times, and we always made sure to take Trevor with us. He might not be the little brother who had needed my help, but that was no reason to leave him out of things. We'd even gone out to dinner one night, without Trevor. Voldar thoughtfully picked a restaurant without any local specialties on the menu.

Speaking of food, I persuaded the cook at the inn to let me bake some brownies for Ahmla. Ahmla said they were the best thing she had ever eaten, and I promised to keep her stocked with care packages of them when I got home. Brownies are one thing you just can't make over a fireplace.

My father had finished writing his magazine article and sent it in to his editor. She liked it so much that she promised Dad the chance to write more travel pieces in the future. "Maybe we'll get to go to Paris next," he said hopefully.

"No, Copenhagen!" said Trevor. "Then I could go to Legoland."

Our Drazylvonian Christmas had turned out to be lots of fun, too. We had spent it with Voldar's family, and they'd gone to a lot of trouble to prepare us a "typical American" Christmas dinner. Although none of us had ever seen or tasted foods even remotely like them in the United States, we appreciated the effort.

For Christmas, by the way, Trevor got so much Lego stuff that I was pretty sure our plane would have trouble on the way home, too. I don't know where my parents had hidden it all. Maybe they had found a toy store somewhere in Drazylvonia.

"How about leaving your *old* Lego stuff here?" I asked as we were packing. "Maybe some other kid who came here could use it. It would be a nice surprise for him."

"Yeah, right," said Trevor scornfully. "If he tries it, I'll pound him into the ground."

"Trevor!" Mom protested. "That's not a nice thing to say."

"Well, then, I'll *slap* him into the ground," said my brother sweetly.

"I have enjoyed our time together," said Voldar formally, looking up at the airport wall. It was finally time to leave. I had dreaded my trip here, but now I didn't want to go home.

"I had a good time, too," I said, looking down at the floor.

"You have packed my address?" Voldar asked.

"Of course. Wait, do you have mine? Here, I'll give it to you—"

"You have already done so three or four times," Voldar told me.

"Oh. Okay. Well, then you have my address. So you can write me if anything exciting happens around here."

"I have the feeling that with you gone, life will seem rather ordinary," said Voldar.

Was that a compliment? I hoped so.

"Okay, Meg. They're boarding our row," my father said behind us. "You'd better say goodbye."

Before Voldar and I could say anything at all, Trevor peered up into our faces. "Aren't you going to *kiss*?" he asked. "Mom said it was so *cute* the way you guys were spending so much time together!"

That did it. "I will write you, Meg," said Voldar in a strangled voice. And he bolted from the airport as if all the vampires in Drazylvonia were chasing him.

I turned to Trevor and announced, between clenched teeth, that he had better get his butt onto the plane before I pounded *him* into the ground.

No vampires turned up on the plane on the way home, although the woman across the aisle from me was, like the one coming over, loud and obnoxious. I guess that's just my fate on airplanes.

After we had gotten home and gotten reacquainted with Pooch (who had been fed so well by the house sitter that he had completely stopped caring about us) and opened all the mail (I got one catalogue and three chain letters—yuck!) , I dragged my suitcase upstairs to my room.

"And please unpack right away," Mom called up the stairs after me. "I don't want your stuff getting moldy."

I sighed heavily as the suitcase and I clumped into my bedroom. As long as your suitcase is still closed, you can fool yourself into thinking your vacation isn't over yet.

But I didn't want to get into an argument with my mother this soon after we'd gotten home. So I unzipped my suitcase—

And a sprig of death's-head thyme fell to the ground.

"No," I whispered. "Oh, no. Please."

It hadn't been there when I had packed. I *knew* it hadn't. The only death's-head thyme I had ever seen was now clutched in the hand of a headless vampire in fallen Castle Vladestan. So how had this gotten here?

I didn't know. But I knew it carried a message from someone in Castle Vladestan.

Back to normal old real life. Right.

I had the feeling that my life would never be normal again.

ANN HODGMAN is a former children's book editor and the author of over forty children's books, including the popular *My Babysitter Is a Vampire* series and the *Stinky Stanley* series. In addition to humorous fiction for children, she has written teen mysteries and nonfiction for reluctant readers. She lives with her husband, two children, and seventeen pets in Washington, Connecticut.

JOHN PIERARD has illustrated the bestselling *My Teacher Is an Alien* series and the *My Babysitter Is a Vampire* series. His pictures can also be found in several books in the *Time Machine* series and in *Isaac Asimov's Science Fiction* Magazine. He lives in Manhattan.